"It's just you. Only you, Lizzie."

That was the right answer. She rubbed her temples, thinking that this felt a lot like a relationship. It really did. Part of her wanted to fight falling into it. Part of her couldn't stop.

"Are you free tomorrow night? My brother's in town for a preseason game. You want to come with me?"

She loved football. "I don't know."

"Yeah, you do. But you don't trust me."

"Sean, I'm not interested in getting my heart broken."

"Then we have something in common. I'm not interested in breaking your heart."

Dear Reader,

Sean O'Banyon, barely reformed bad boy turned Wall Street business mogul, first showed up in THE MOOREHOUSE LEGACY (*His Comfort and Joy*, Special Edition #1732). In Sean's very first scene, he ended up giving his good buddy Gray Bennett a hard time for falling in love—and as I wrote his cheeky dialogue, I thought, *Oh, you're going to get yours, big guy! Just you wait!*

Well, I'm happy to say that Sean definitely got his, so to speak...in the form of the wonderful and caring Lizzie Bond. Lizzie is the only woman who could possibly get through Sean's defenses. She's caring and kind, but no pushover—so she holds him accountable for his actions and emotions in a way no one else has. The two of them are great together!

I hope you enjoy reading about Sean and Lizzie as much as I enjoyed writing about them—they are a very special pair. As always, I would love to hear from you! E-mail me at Jessica@JessicaBird.com.

Happy reading!

Jessica

THE
BILLIONAIRE
NEXT DOOR

JESSICA BIRD

SPECIAL EDITION®

Published by Silhouette Books

America's Publisher of Contemporary Romance

SILHOUETTE BOOKS

ISBN-13: 978-0-373-24844-5
ISBN-10:   0-373-24844-X

THE BILLIONAIRE NEXT DOOR

Copyright © 2007 by Jessica Bird

Visit Silhouette Books at www.eHarlequin.com

Printed in U.S.A.

Books by Jessica Bird

Silhouette Special Edition

*Beauty and the Black Sheep #1698
*His Comfort and Joy #1732
*From the First #1750
*A Man in a Million #1803
†The Billionaire Next Door #1844

*The Moorehouse Legacy
†The O'Banyon Brothers

JESSICA BIRD

graduated from college with a double major in history and art history, concentrating in the medieval period, which meant she was great at discussing anything that happened before the sixteenth century, but not all that employable in the real world. In order to support herself, she went to law school and worked in Boston in health care administration for many years.

She now lives in the South with her husband and her beloved golden retriever. As a writer, her commute is a heck of a lot better than it was as a lawyer, and she's thrilled that her professional wardrobe includes slippers and sweatpants. She likes to write love stories that feature strong, independent heroines and complex, alpha male heroes. Visit her Web site at www.JessicaBird.com and e-mail her at Jessica@JessicaBird.com.

For my family, with love

Chapter One

"No, really, I heard he was coming tonight."

The young investment banker looked at his buddy, Freddie Wilcox. "O'Banyon? Are you crazy? He's in the middle of the Condi-Foods merger."

"I asked his assistant." Freddie tweaked his Hermès tie. "It's on his calendar."

"He must never sleep."

"Gods don't have to, Andrew."

"Well, then, where is he?"

From their vantage point in a corner of the Waldorf-Astoria's ballroom, they sifted through the crowd of Manhattan highfliers, looking for the man they called The Idol.

Sean O'Banyon was their boss's boss and, at thirty-six, one of Wall Street's big dogs. He ran the mergers-and-acquisitions arm of Sterling Rochester, and was capable of leveraging billions of dollars at the drop of a hat or killing a mega deal because he didn't like the numbers. Since arriving on the Street, he'd engineered one perfectly executed corporate acquisition after another. No one had his track record or his instincts.

Or his reputation for eating hard-core financiers for lunch.

Man, folks would have called him SOB even if those hadn't been his initials.

He was indeed a god, but he was also a thorn in the side of the I-banking world's old-school types. O'Banyon was from South Boston, not Greenwich. Drove a Maserati not a Mercedes. Didn't care about people's *Mayflower* roots or European pedigrees. With no family money to speak of, he'd gone to Harvard undergrad on scholarship, got his start at JP Morgan then put himself through Harvard Business School while doing deals as a consultant.

Word had it that when he lost his temper, his Southie accent came back.

So, yes, the white-shoe, country-club set couldn't stand him…at least not until they needed him to find financing for their corporations' expansion plans or share buy-backs. O'Banyon was the master at drumming up money. In addition to all the bank funds at his disposal, he had ins with some serious private sources like the great Nick Farrell or the now-governor of Massachusetts, Jack Walker.

O'Banyon was who everyone wanted to be. A rebel

with immense power. An iconoclast with guts and glory. The Idol.

"Oh…my God, it's him."

Andrew whipped his head around.

Sean O'Banyon walked into the ballroom as if he owned the place. And not just the Waldorf, all of New York City. Dressed in a spectacular pin-striped black suit and wearing a screaming red tie, he was sporting a cynical half grin. As per usual.

"He's wearing all Gucci. Must have cost him five grand before tailoring."

"Couch change. I heard he spent a quarter million dollars on a watch last year."

"It was a half million. I checked at Tourneau."

O'Banyon's hair was as dark as his suit and his face was nothing but hard-ass angles and arched eyebrows. And his build matched his attitude. He topped out at six-four and it wasn't padding that filled out his shoulders. Rumor had it he did triathlons for kicks and giggles.

As the crowd caught sight of him, a swarm condensed and closed in, people pumping his hand, clapping him on the shoulder, smiling. He kept walking, the powerbrokers and A-listers forming his wake.

"He's coming over here," Andrew hissed.

"Oh God, is my tie okay?"

"Yeah. Is mine—"

"Fine."

"I think I'm going to crap in my pants."

Lizzie Bond stared at the stripped hospital bed and thought of the man who'd lain in it these last six days.

The heart monitor he'd been on and the IV that he'd needed and the oxygen feed were all gone. So too the cardiac crash cart that had failed to revive him forty-two minutes ago.

Eddie O'Banyon was dead at the age of sixty-four. And he had died alone.

She shifted her eyes to a window that overlooked Boston's Charles River.

As a nurse, she was accustomed to being in patient rooms, used to the tangy smell of disinfectant and the bland walls and the air of quiet desperation. But she had come to this room as a friend, not as a health-care professional, so she was seeing things through different eyes.

Like how empty and quiet it was.

She glanced back to the bed. She hated that Mr. O'Banyon had died alone.

She'd wanted to be at his side, had promised him she would be, but when the final myocardial infarction had occurred, she'd been working at the health clinic in Roxbury all the way across town. So she had missed saying goodbye. And he had dealt with whatever pain that had come to claim him by himself.

When the call that he had passed came through to her, she'd left her day job immediately and screamed through traffic to get here. Even though the dead had no schedules to keep and he would never know if she'd hadn't rushed, it had seemed right to hurry.

"Lizzie?"

Lizzie turned around. The nurse standing in the doorway was someone she knew and liked. "Hi, Teresa."

"I have his things from when he came in. They were still in the ED."

"Thanks for bringing them up."

Lizzie accepted her friend's personal effects with a sad smile. The plastic bag was transparent, so she could see the well-worn robe and the plaid pajamas Mr. O'Banyon had had on when he'd been admitted around 1:00 a.m. last Sunday.

What a horrible night that had been, the beginning of the end. He'd called her around twelve with chest pains and she'd run up the duplex's stairs to his apartment. Though he'd been her landlord for two years, he was also a friend and she'd had to call on all her professional training to keep sharp and make the right decision about what to do for him. In the end, she'd called 911 over his objections and not let herself be swayed. The paramedics had come quickly and she'd insisted on riding in the ambulance with Mr. O'Banyon even though he'd tried to tell her he didn't need the help.

Which had been so like him. Always irascible, always a loner. But he had needed her. His eyes had watered from fear the whole trip from South Boston to Mass General in Beacon Hill and he'd held on to her hand until her fingers had gone numb. It was as if he'd known he wouldn't be going back out into the world again.

"I know you were the emergency contact," Teresa said, "but does he have any next of kin?"

"A son. He wouldn't let me call him though. Said only if something happened." And something certainly had.

"You'll get in touch with the son, then? Because unless you're going to claim the body…"

"I'll make the call."

Teresa came over and squeezed Lizzie's shoulder. "Are you okay?"

"I should have been here."

"You were. In spirit." When she started to shake her head, Teresa cut in, "There was no way you could have known."

"I just... He was alone. I didn't want him to be alone."

"Lizzie, you always take such good care of everybody. Remember in nursing school when I fell apart three weeks before graduation? I never would have made it without you."

Lizzie smiled a little. "You would have been fine."

"Don't underestimate how much you helped me." Teresa went back to the door. "Listen, let me or one of the other girls know if you or that son of his need anything, okay?"

"Will do. Thanks, Teresa."

After the other nurse left, Lizzie put the plastic bag on the bare mattress and rifled around until she found a battered wallet. As she opened the leather billfold, she told herself that she wasn't invading Mr. O'Banyon's privacy. But it still didn't feel right.

The piece of paper she eventually took out was folded four times and as flat as a pressed leaf, as if it had been in there for quite a while. There was one name on it and a number with a 212 area code.

Guess his son lived in Manhattan.

Lizzie sat down on the bed and took her cell phone out of her purse.

Except she couldn't call just yet. She had to stitch herself back together a little. At the moment, she felt like a stuffed animal whose side had been torn open and whose padding was leaking.

She glanced back at the bag and was overcome with grief.

Over the past two years, Mr. O'Banyon had become a kind of surrogate father to her. Gruff, prickly and standoffish in the beginning, he'd stayed that way...but only on the surface. As time had passed and his health had declined, he'd gotten as attached to her as she was to him, always asking her when she was coming back to see him, always worried about her driving after dark, always keeping up with how her day went or what she was thinking about. As his heart had grown weaker and weaker, their ties had grown stronger and stronger. Gradually, she'd done more things for him, buying groceries, doing errands, cleaning up, helping him keep all his doctor's appointments straight.

She'd liked being responsible for him. With no husband or children of her own, and a mother who was too fey to really connect with, Lizzie's caretaking nature had needed an outlet beyond her job. Mr. O'Banyon had been it.

Clear as day, she pictured him sitting in his Barcalounger in front of his TV, a crossword puzzle balanced on the arm of the chair, his reading glasses down on his nose. He had been so sad and lonely, not that he'd ever shown that outright. It was just...well, Lizzie was a little sad and lonely, too, so she'd recognized the shadows in his eyes as exactly what she saw in her own mirror.

And now he was gone.

She stared down at her cell phone and the piece of paper she'd taken out of his wallet. His son's name was Sean, evidently.

She started to dial, but then stopped, picked up the bag of Mr. O'Banyon's things and headed out.

When she talked to the man's son, she was going to need some fresh air.

Standing in the Waldorf's ballroom, Sean O'Banyon smiled at Marshall Williamson III and thought about how the guy had tried to blackball him at the Congress Club. Hadn't worked, but good old Williamson had given it his best shot.

"You're the pinnacle," Williamson was saying. "Without peer. You are the man I want on this merger."

Sean smiled and figured that given the amount of groveling that was going on, Williamson was remembering the blackball thing, too.

"Thanks, Marshall. You call my assistant. She'll get you in to see me."

"Thank *you*, Sean. After all you did for Trolly Construction, I know you—"

"Call my assistant." Sean clapped Marshall on the shoulder to cut him off because getting stroked was boring. Especially when the sucking up was insincere and business motivated. "I'm going to get a drink. I'll see you sometime next week."

As he turned away, he was still smiling. Watching men who'd cut him down eat their pride made up for the social slights he had to deal with. Thing was, there was one and only one golden rule on Wall Street: He who had the gold, or could get it, made the rules. And in spite of his nothing-doing background, Sean was a mine for that shiny yellow stuff.

While he headed for the bar, he looked around the ballroom and saw the crowd for exactly what they were. He was under no illusions that any of these people were his friends. They were his allies or his enemies and sometimes both at the same time. Or they were acquaintances who wanted to have their pictures taken with him. Or they were women who'd been his lovers.

But there was no one here he was particularly close to. And he liked it that way.

"Hello, Sean."

He glanced to his left and thought, ah, yes, a bridal barracuda. "Hello, Candace."

The blonde sidled up to him, all pouty lips and big, insincere eyes. She was dressed in a black gown that was so low cut you could almost see her belly button, and her surgically enhanced assets were displayed as if they were up for sale. Which he supposed they were. For the right engagement ring and a generous prenup, Candace would walk down the aisle with a bridge troll.

Her voice was slightly breathless as she spoke. Possibly because of all the silicone on top of her lungs. "I heard you were out in the Hamptons last weekend. You didn't call."

"Busy. Sorry."

She pressed herself against him. "You need to call me when you're there. Actually, you just need to call me."

He disengaged himself as if he were peeling free of a coat. "Like I told you a while ago, I'm not your type."

"I disagree."

"Haven't you heard about me?"

"Of course. I read about you in the *Wall Street Journal* all the time."

"Ah, that's business, though. Let me enlighten you about the personal side of things." He leaned down and whispered in her ear, "I never buy jewelry for women. Or cars or plane tickets or clothes or houses or hotel rooms. And I believe in splitting the check over dinner. Right down to the tip."

She hauled back as if he'd blasphemed.

He smiled. "I see you get my point. Trust me, you'll be much happier with someone else."

As he turned away from her and walked over to the bar, he had to laugh. The thing was, he hadn't said those things just to get rid of her. They were the God's honest truth: For him, Dutch was the rule with women.

The minute he'd made his first big chunk of cash, he'd become a target for that kind of predatory female and he'd gotten burned. Back over a decade ago, after having lived for years as the poor relation to his room-mates and friends at Harvard, he'd finally put together a deal with a percentage point or two in it for him.

The cash had been an avalanche. More than he could ever have imagined filling his account. And within a week of him throwing some of it around, a very sophis-ticated blonde, not unlike Candace, had shown up on his doorstep. She'd been everything he'd ever wanted, proof positive that he'd arrived. Elegant, cultured, an antiques dealer with style, he'd felt invincible with her on his arm.

He'd done his best to buy her anything she wanted and she'd been more than happy to trade her presence for the things he got her. At least until she'd found someone who could write even bigger checks. On her way out the door, she'd told him, in her Upper East Side, long-voweled way, that even though he was just a roughneck from South Boston, she could tell he was going places…so he should never hesitate to call her if he was ever in the market for oil paintings.

Lesson learned.

Now, it was easy to pick out women like that, although not because he was a genius at reading minds. Pretty much anyone he met in a dress was after money.

Just like anyone in a suit, too, come to think of it.

After he ordered a Tanqueray and tonic from the bartender, he noticed two young guys edging their way over to him. They were dressed well, real spit and polish, Ivy League shiny, and their faces were composed as if they were prepared to play it cool.

Except both of them were rubbing their right palms on their hips as if they were worried they'd offer him a wet handshake.

"'Evening, Mr. O'Banyon," the taller one said.

Sean got his T&T and pointed to the guy. "Fred Wilcox. And…Andrew Frick, right?"

The two nodded their heads, clearly astounded he knew their names. But you had to keep up with the FNUGs. Some percentage of them were going to make it and thus become useful, and besides, he liked the look of this pair. Smart eyes, but none of that showboat crap some of the other young hardies tried to pull. Plus, if he remembered correctly, they were both HBS like him.

"How you boys doing tonight?" he said.

They stammered over some social nonsense then fell completely silent as a cloud of perfume wafted in. Sean glanced behind his shoulder and then smiled honestly for the first time since walking into the gala.

"My lovely, Elena," he murmured, leaning down and kissing the smooth cheek of a stunning brunette. As she greeted him in Italian and he replied, he could positively feel the hero worship coming at him from the young guys. He glanced at them. "Will you excuse us?"

"Of course, Mr. O'Banyon."

"Absolutely, Mr. O'Banyon."

"Wait up," he said on impulse as they turned away. "You two want in on some fun?"

Frick blinked. "Ah, yes, sir."

"Call my assistant tomorrow morning. She'll put you in touch with the Condi-Food analysts and they'll find you a little slice of the deal to work on. Don't worry about your boss. I'll call Harry and tell him you're going to come play with me for a while."

As their eyes bugged as if they'd been goosed by a pair of pliers, Sean smiled. Man, he remembered what that felt like. To be young and green and desperate to be given a shot at the big time…and have a door opened.

The thank-yous from them started to roll fast as marbles on a bare floor. "No problem," Sean said, then narrowed his eyes. "Just stay tight and use your brains and everything will be fine."

He turned his attention to Elena. She looked very beautiful tonight, dressed in a red sheath with her hair up high on her head. Rubies glowed from her neck and her earlobes.

"Sean," she said with her lovely accent, "I have a favor to ask you."

"What, baby?" As she smiled, he had to imagine that no one ever called her *baby*. She was a descendent of the Medicis and as rich as her ancestors had been back in the Middle Ages. The thing was, though, in spite of her bloodline and her money, she was a very nice person. They'd met years ago and had shared an immediate, mutual respect.

"Excuse me," one of the photographers cut in. "May I take a picture?"

Sean flipped into social mode, gathering Elena against him and staring into the lens. There was a flash, a thank-you from the guy, and then he and Elena went back to their conversation.

"What kind of favor do you need?" Sean asked.

"An escort to the Hall Foundation Gala."

Oh, okay, he knew what this was all about. Her recent marital separation had been messy and public and had involved infidelity on her husband's side. To top it off, the guy was trying to suck tens of millions of dollars out of her in the divorce…despite the fact that he was still with the masseuse he'd gotten pregnant.

The details of the split had been written up in *Vanity Fair* and *New York Magazine,* but that wasn't the worst of it. Everyone on the A-list circuit was talking about what had happened and not with kindness. They were whispering that Elena had gone out and bought herself a younger man then hadn't been able to keep him. And that he'd wandered because she couldn't have children. And that Elena was a cold fish.

Sean didn't know about the kids part, but he was certain that she'd been passionately in love with her husband when they'd gotten married. Too bad everyone else seemed to have forgotten that.

God, Manhattan could be a very cold place even if you lived in a penthouse on Park Avenue with perfectly good heating and ventilation. All it took was for your private life to become the scandal du jour and you became fodder, not friend. And gossip was like chum to the social sharks, sure to attract a frenzy.

If Elena didn't show up at the Hall Foundation Gala? She'd look as if she were weak and that would only incite the harping more. But if she arrived at the event with him, she'd appear strong and desirable.

He reached out and took her hand. "I'm there for you. One hundred percent."

She positively sagged with relief. "Thank you. This has been a very difficult time."

He pulled her forward and tucked her into his body as a friend or a brother would, for comfort. "You don't worry about a thing."

When his phone started to ring in his breast pocket, he took it out. The 617 area code made him frown because he didn't recognize the rest of the caller's number.

"I'll let you take that," Elena said, kissing him on the cheek. "And seriously, Sean…thank you."

"Don't go, baby. This'll just take a sec." He accepted the call. "Yeah?"

The pause that followed was broken by the wail of an ambulance siren. Then a female voice said, "Sean O'Banyon?"

"Who is this and how did you get this number?"

"My name is Elizabeth Bond. I got it from your voice mail. I'm…I'm so very sorry to tell you this…but your father has passed."

All at once, the sounds of the party drained away. The patter of talk, the winding chords of the chamber orchestra, the trilling laughter of a woman nearby—all of it disappeared as if someone had thrown a thick blanket over everything. And then the sight of the 150 people before him fogged out until he was alone in the vast room.

In fact, the very fabric of reality disintegrated until it seemed as if the world had become an intangible dreamscape and him a formless vapor: he couldn't feel the floor under his feet or the phone in his palm or the weight of his body. Nor could he remember what he was doing in this room full of crystal chandeliers and too much perfume.

"When?" The heavy word came out of his mouth without benefit of conscious thought.

"Less than an hour ago. He suffered a second heart attack."

"When was the first?"

"Six days ago."

"Six days ago?" he asked in an utterly level tone.

There was a hesitation, as if the woman on the other end was unsure what his mental state was. Funny, that made two of them.

She cleared her throat. "Immediately following his first, he was taken by ambulance here to Mass General, and though he was revived, the damage to his heart muscle was extensive. Following an angiogram, it was revealed that he had multiple blockages, but he was not stable enough for surgery."

Dimly, Sean heard the sound of ice tinkling in a glass and he looked down. His hand was shaking so badly his Tanqueray and tonic might as well have been in a blender. He leaned to the side and put the drink down on a table.

"What happens to him now?" he asked, shoving his hand in his pocket.

"He will be held here at Mass General until the family makes arrangements." When he didn't respond, she said, "Mr. O'Banyon? Will you be making arrangements? Um…hello?"

"Yes, I will. I'll fly up tonight. What do I need to do once I'm at the hospital?" As she proceeded to tell him who to call and where to go at MGH, he wasn't tracking. The only thing that stuck was that he could phone the general information number if he needed help or had further questions.

"I'm very sorry," the woman said and she obviously meant it. There was true sorrow in her voice. "I—"

"Are you a nurse?"

"Yes, I am. But your father wasn't a patient of mine. He was—"

"Thank you for calling me. If you'll excuse me, I need to make some calls. Goodbye."

He hung up and stared at his phone. Obviously his father had listed him as next of kin, which explained how the woman had gotten the number.

"Sean? Is everything all right?"

He glanced at Elena. It took a moment or two for him to recognize her, but eventually her worried mahogany eyes got through to him. "My father is dead."

As she gasped and put her hand on his arm, a booming voice barreled through the crowd at them. "Sean O'Banyon, as I live and breathe!"

Sean turned to see the owner of a shipping conglomerate lumbering over like a bear through the woods. The man was as ungainly as the mega-ton freight haulers he put out on the oceans and he had the mouth of a longshoreman. In typical Manhattan fashion, he was welcome here tonight only because he'd given five million dollars to the cause.

"I'll handle him," Elena whispered. "You, go now."

Sean nodded and took off, heading for the back exit while trying to dodge all the people who wanted things from him. As he fought through the crowd, he felt as if he couldn't breathe and a curious panic set in.

When he finally burst outside through a fire door, he had to lean down and put his hands on his knees. Drawing the sultry summer air down his throat and into his lungs only made the suffocation worse and he wrenched at his tie.

Dead. His father was dead.

He and his brothers were finally free.

Sean forced himself to stand up like a man and pushed a hand through his hair to try and clear his brain. Yeah…freedom had come with that phone call.

Hadn't it?

Tilting his head back, he measured the lack of stars in the sky and thought about the inflection in the nurse's words, the sadness and the regret.

How appropriate that the person mourning his father was a stranger.

God knew, his sons would never be able to.

Chapter Two

Lizzie hung up her cell phone and stared at the thing. Through the din of what sounded like a party, Mr. O'Banyon's son had been totally detached, his voice giving away no emotion at all. Then again, she was a stranger and the news had not been good or expected. He was no doubt in shock.

She'd wanted to find out when and where the funeral would be held, but that hadn't seemed like an appropriate thing to bring up. Worst came to worst she could always call him later.

An ambulance went by her, its lights flashing red and white, its siren letting out a single squawk as it left the Mass General complex and headed out onto Cambridge Avenue. The sight of it got her moving and she started for the parking garage. Part of her wanted to stay here and wait for the son to arrive, but it would take him hours to get into town. Plus it appeared that he was the type who'd rather deal with things on his own.

Besides, it was time to go to her second job.

Lizzie jogged across the road and took two flights of concrete stairs up to the second story of the garage. When she found her old Toyota Camry in the lines of cars, she unlocked it with a key as the remote no longer worked, and put Mr. O'Banyon's things on the back-seat. Getting behind the wheel, she figured she'd leave the bag by the upstairs apartment's door for the son along with a note that if there was anything she could do to help she was always available.

The drive from Beacon Hill to Chinatown took her on a straight shot up Charles Street, then a jog around the Commons, followed by a scoot past Emerson College. Down farther, opposite one of the Big Dig's gaping mouths, was Boston Medical Center. Affiliated with Boston University, BMC was a busy urban hospital and its emergency department saw a lot of action. Particularly, and tragically, of the gunshot and stabbing variety.

She'd been moonlighting in the ED three nights a week for the past year because, though she worked days at the health clinic in Roxbury, she needed the extra income. Her mother lived in an artist's world of color and texture and not much reality, so Lizzie helped her out a lot, covering her expenses, paying bills, making sure she had enough money. To Alma Bond, the world was a place of beauty and magic; practical matters rarely permeated her fog of inspiration.

The extra income was also for Lizzie, however. Earlier in the year, she'd applied and been accepted into a master's program for public health. Though she couldn't afford to start this fall, her plan was to save up over the next few months and matriculate in the winter session.

Except now she wondered whether she needed to find a new place to live. Would Mr. O'Banyon's son hold on to the duplex? If he sold it, would her new landlord ask for more in rent? How would she find something equally inexpensive?

After driving through BMC's parking garage, Lizzie squeezed the Toyota in between two mountain-size SUVs and took a last look at Mr. O'Banyon's things. Then she got out, locked the car and strode toward the bank of elevators.

As she waited for the metal doors to slide open, Sean O'Banyon's hard tone and emotionless words came back to her.

Maybe that hadn't been shock. Maybe that had been genuine disregard.

God, what could cause a father and son to lose touch to such a degree?

It was 3:16 in the morning when Sean stopped his rental car in front of the Southie row house where he and his brothers had grown up.

The duplex looked exactly the same: two stories of nothing special sided in an ugly pale blue. Front porch was a shallow lip of a thing, more a landing than a place to sit outside. Upstairs was all dark. Downstairs had what looked like a single lamp on in the living room.

He wondered who was staying in the bottom unit now. They'd always rented it out and clearly that was still the practice.

With a twist of his wrist, Sean turned the engine off, took the key out of the ignition then eased back in the seat.

On the flight from Teterboro to Logan, he'd made two phone calls, both of which had dumped into voice mail. The first had been to his younger brother, Billy, who was traveling around to preseason games with the rest of the New England Patriots football team. The second was to an international exchange that was the only way he had to get in touch with Mac. The oldest O'Banyon boy was a special forces soldier in the U.S. Army so God only knew where he was at any given time.

Sean had told them both to call him back as soon as they got the message.

He looked up to the second story of the house and felt his skin tighten around his bones and muscles. Man, Pavlov had been right about trained responses to stimuli. Even though Sean was a grown man, as he stared at the windows of his childhood apartment, he felt his ten-year-old self's terror.

Dropping his head, he rubbed his eyes. The damn things felt as if they had sawdust in them and his temples were pounding.

But then stress'll do that to you.

He *so* didn't want to go into that house. Probably should have stayed at the Four Seasons, which was what he usually did when he was in town. Except on some molecular level, he needed to see the old place even though he hated it. Needed to go inside.

It was like peeling back a Band-Aid and checking out a cut.

With a curse, he grabbed his leather duffel as well as the two bags of groceries he'd bought at a twenty-four-hour Star Market, then opened the car door and stood up.

Boston smelled different than New York. Always had. Tonight, the brine of the ocean was especially heavy in the air, buffered by the sweet sweat of summer's humidity. As his nose ate up the scent, his brain registered it as home.

He followed the short concrete walkway up to the house then long-legged the five steps to the shallow front porch. He didn't have a key, but as always, there was one tucked behind the flimsy metal mailbox that was tacked onto the aluminum siding.

The door opened with the exact same squeak he remembered, and, hearing the hinge complain, his blood turned into icy slush.

That squeak had always been the warning, the call to listen hard for what came next. If it was a door closing underneath them, he and his brothers would take a deep breath because it was just the tenants coming home. But if it was footsteps on the stairs? That meant pure panic and running for cover.

As he stepped inside the foyer, Sean's heart started to jackrabbit in his chest and sweat broke out on his forehead.

Except, damn it, he was thirty-six years old and the

man was dead. Nothing could hurt him here anymore. Nothing.

Uh-huh, right. Too bad his body didn't know this. As he went up the staircase, his knees were weak and his gut was a lead balloon. And God, the sound of the wood creaking under his soles was awful in his ears. The dirge of his approach was the same as when his father had come home, and hearing his own footsteps now, he remembered the fear he had felt as a boy as the thundering noise grew louder and louder.

At the top of the landing he put his hand on the doorknob and the key in the lock. Before he went in, he told himself this was only a door and he wasn't stepping back into his past. The space-time continuum just didn't work that way. Thank God.

But he was still in a cold sweat as he opened up and walked in.

When he turned on the lights, he was amazed. Everything was exactly the same: the tattered Barcalounger with the TV tray right next to it; the rumpled couch with its faded flower print; the 1970s lamps that were as big as oil drums and just as ugly; the crucifix on the wall, the yellowed, exhausted lace drapery.

The air was stuffy in spite of the air conditioner that was humming, so he cracked open a window. The place smelled of cigarette smoke, but it was the kind of thing left over after a four-pack-a-day addict stops. The stench lingered, embedded in the room's paint and flooring and fabrics, but wasn't in the air itself.

As the breeze came in, he walked over to the TV tray and picked up the *Boston Globe* crossword puzzle that was mostly done. The date in the upper right-hand corner was from the previous Sunday, the last time his father had sat in the chair with a pencil in hand filling in little boxes with wobbly, capitalized letters.

Going by the script, it seemed as if his father had had hand tremors. Odd, to picture him as anything other than brutally strong.

Sean put the paper down and forced himself to walk through every room. It was about halfway through the tour when he realized something was different.

Everything was clean.

The cramped kitchen was tidy, no dirty dishes in the sink, no trash collecting in the Rubbermaid bin in the corner, no food left out on the counters. The room he'd shared with Billy had both beds made and a vacuumed rug. Mac's bedroom was just as neat. Their father's private space was likewise in wilted but tidy condition.

Back when Sean had lived here, there had been cobwebs in the corners of the rooms and dirt tracked in the front door and beds with rumpled sheets and dust everywhere. There had also been a lot of empty bottles.

With a compulsion he couldn't fight, Sean went through all the closets and cupboards and dressers in the apartment. He looked under each bed and the couch. Checked behind the TV and then went into the kitchen and moved the refrigerator out from the wall.

Not one single booze bottle. Not one beer can.

No alcohol in the place.

As he threw his shoulder into the fridge and forced the thing back into place, he was flat-out amazed. He'd never have thought their father could kick the sauce. The drinking had been as much a part of him as his dark hair and the hard tone of his voice.

Sean stalled out, but then went into the living room and figured it was time to score some shut-eye. First thing tomorrow, he was going to make arrangements with Finnegan's Funeral Home for the cremation and the interment. After that, he'd have to pack up the apartment. No question they would sell the duplex. There was no reason to come back here ever again.

He glanced around. God, how long had it been since he'd stood in this room?

As he went through the years, he was surprised to realize it had been all the way back when he'd gone away to Harvard as a freshman. Made sense though. College had been his ticket out, and once he didn't have to sleep under this roof, he'd made damn sure he never showed up again. It had been the same for Billy when he'd gotten a football scholarship to Holy Cross. And for Mac, who'd joined the army the very month Billy went off to college. They'd all left and never returned.

Go figure.

Sean went over to his duffel, stripped down to his boxers and grabbed his toothbrush. After he hit the bathroom in the hall, he picked a pillow off his old bed and headed for the couch.

No way in hell he was sleeping in his room.

Lying flat on his back in the dark, he thought of the penthouse he lived in down in Manhattan. Park Avenue in the seventies, a perfect address. And everything in that showstopper of a place was sleek and expensive, from the furniture to the drapes to the kitchen appliances to that million-dollar view of Central Park.

It was about as far away from where he was now as was humanly possible.

Sean screwed his lids down, crossed his arms over his chest and concentrated on going to sleep.

Yeah, right.

He lasted not even ten minutes before he was on his bare feet and pacing up and down over the knobby area rug.

Lizzie parked the Toyota in front of the row house and got out with the bag of Mr. O'Banyon's things. Her feet were killing her and she had a headache from having had too many coffees, but at least she didn't have to be at the clinic until noon today because she was working the later shift.

As she stepped onto the duplex's concrete walkway, she stopped and looked up. No lights were on upstairs, but that wasn't because someone was sleeping. It was because no one lived there anymore.

Tears stung her eyes. It was hard to imagine her cranky old friend gone. Hard to internalize the fact that there would be no more blue glow from his TV at night, no more sound of him shuffling about, no more trips to buy him the chocolate ice cream he liked.

No more talking to him the way a daughter talked to a gruff father.

She tightened her grip on the bag's handles and hoped he hadn't struggled at the end, hadn't felt horrible pain and fear. She wished for him a peaceful slide as he passed, not a bumpy, frightening fall.

As she went up to the house, she felt as if there was a draft licking around her body, as if the night had turned frigid though it was in fact balmy.

It was just so hard to come home this morning. To her, there was only empty space above her now. The man whose life had animated the furniture and the objects in the other apartment was gone and the silence overhead was only going to remind her of what had been lost.

After Lizzie let herself into her place, she put her keys in a dish on her little painted table and shut the door. She was setting down the plastic bag when she froze.

Someone was walking around upstairs.

Her first thought was totally illogical: for a split second, she was sure that someone had made a mistake with Mr. O'Banyon and he'd been discharged because he was perfectly healthy.

Her second thought was that a burglar had broken in.

Except then she realized whoever it was was pacing. Back. Forth. Back. Forth.

The son had come into town.

She started for the door, but then stopped because going up to see him was ridiculous. Though she'd been close to the guy's father, she didn't know the son at all and it was just before dawn, for heaven's sake. Hardly the time for a sympathy call.

After she took a shower, she sat in her living room with a bowl of corn flakes in her lap. Instead of eating the cereal, she played with it until it turned to mush, and listened to the man above her wear out the floorboards.

Twenty minutes later, she put on a pair of jeans and went up the stairwell.

The moment she knocked, the pacing stopped. Just in case *he* thought she was a burglar, she said, "Hello? Mr.—ah, Sean O'Banyon?"

Nothing could have prepared her for who opened that door.

The man on the other side of the jamb stood about six inches taller than her and wore nothing but a pair of boxers and a whole lot of muscle. With a gold cross hanging from his neck, an old tattoo on his left pec and a scar on one of his shoulders, he looked a little dangerous…especially in the face. His hazel eyes were sharp as razors, his jaw set as if he was used to being in charge, his lips nothing but a tight, hard line.

She could totally imagine the cold tone she'd heard over her phone coming out of that mouth.

"Yeah?" His voice was very deep.

"I'm Lizzie—Elizabeth Bond. I talked to you today—yesterday. I live downstairs."

All at once his face eased up. "Ah, hell. I'm making too much noise, aren't I? Worse, I've been at it for a while." His South Boston accent flattened out his vowels and sharpened his consonants. Funny, she hadn't noticed the intonation over the phone, but it was clear as day now. And she'd seen him somewhere. Then again, it was probably because he looked like his father.

"Anyway," he said, "I'm sorry and I'll cut it out."

"Oh, that wasn't why I came up. And I just got home

from my shift so I missed most of the pacing." She took a deep breath and smelled...whoa, a very nice cologne. "I'm truly sorry about your loss and I—"

"Hey, you want some breakfast?"

"Excuse me?"

"Breakfast." As he pushed a hand through his thick dark hair, his bicep flexed up and the gleaming cross shifted between his pecs. "I'm not going to sleep anytime soon and I'm hungry."

"Oh...well...that's not necessary."

"Of course it isn't. But you just got home from work, didn't you?"

"Ah, yes."

"So you're probably hungry, too, right?"

Come to think of it she was.

"And I'll even put my pants on for you, Elizabeth."

Absurdly, a rush went through her. And she had the illicit, inappropriate thought that while he was making love to a woman, his voice would sound fantastic in the ear.

God, how could she even think like that?

"Lizzie," she said, walking in. "I go by Lizzie."

Sean tracked the woman as she went by him, very aware of her smooth, gliding stride. Tall and lean, she was wearing an old pair of blue jeans and a four-sizes-too-big Red Sox T-shirt he was willing to bet she'd be sleeping in later. Her shoulder-length blond hair was pulled back in a no-nonsense way and the ends were damp as if she'd just showered. She smelled of Ivory soap.

Which he liked.

"Lizzie it is, then," he said as he closed the door. "And you can call me Sean, of course."

As he spoke, he realized his Southie accent had re-surfaced and it was strange to hear the speech pattern of his childhood back in his words again. During his years at Harvard, he'd assiduously tamed the telltale *r*s and learned a different, less regional way of talking.

Less regional. Ha. Try more upper-class.

Lizzie stopped in the middle of the room, her pale green stare going over everything as if she were inspecting the place. She had smart eyes, he thought.

"So you're a nurse?" he said.

"I am, but I wasn't treating your father. I was a friend of his."

Had he heard that right? "A friend."

"Yes. I've lived downstairs for the past two years so we got to know each other. He was lonely."

"Was he."

"Very." As she nodded, she ran her hand over the back of the Barcalounger. "We had dinner together a lot."

For some reason, the sight of her touching his father's chair creeped him out.

"Well, then, I guess you know the way to the kitchen." Sean reached into his duffel for some jeans. "You mind if I don't put on a shirt? Damn hot up here."

He was surprised when she blushed. "Oh…no. I mean, yes, that's fine."

As she headed out of the room, he pulled on his pants and thought of his father.

Lonely. Yeah, right. Not with this tenant around.

Eddie O'Banyon had been a loner by nature, but it was funny how a pretty young woman could get a man to feeling sociable.

And she'd obviously spent a lot of time up here. Not only did she know where the kitchen was, but along the way, she shifted the edge of a cheap picture that had tilted off center and straightened a pile of mail. He had the feeling she was the reason the place was so clean.

While Sean worked his way up his button fly, he was willing to bet she was also the reason his father had gotten off the booze, too. Nothing like love or some serious attraction to the opposite sex to turn a guy around. At least temporarily.

Except what had she seen in him?

Sean cursed under his breath. Like he had to even ask that? On impulse, he removed his gold watch and tucked it into his duffel. If she'd been attracted to what little cash his father had had, there was no reason for her to know he was swimming in the stuff.

As he went into the kitchen, he wondered if she knew who he was. He figured chances were fifty/fifty. His face had been in the newspapers often enough, but it was the kind of thing that, unless you were into the world of high finance, you'd probably overlook. Although maybe his father had mentioned something.

Not that Eddie had known much.

"So cop a seat and I'll cook for you," Sean said, nodding to the table in the center of the room. "All I got are eggs and bacon, but the good thing is that's hard to screw up."

"Sounds perfect."

He went to where the frying pan had always been kept and what do you know, the thing was still there. "Scrambled okay?"

"Fine."

As he got the bacon going and grabbed the eggs out of the fridge, he kept his tone casual. "So you knew my old man well, huh?"

"He was very kind to me."

I'll bet. "You lived here two years, you said?"

"Since I got out of nursing school. I wasn't around much as I work at a clinic in Roxbury and I moonlight at BMC a lot, but we spent some time together." A sad smile lifted her mouth. "Your father always said I worked too hard."

Did he? What a prince. "And you took care of this place, too, didn't you? I mean, it's pretty obvious. He never was into housekeeping when I knew him."

"Well, at first he wouldn't let me. But after a while, he needed help." She cleared her throat. "When was the last time you saw him? If you don't mind my asking."

"A while. He told you not to call me until it was over, right?"

As she stayed quiet, he cracked eggs into a bowl and started to beat them with a fork. The choppy, liquid sound cut through her silence.

He looked over his shoulder. "Didn't he?"

"Yes. It felt wrong not to, but I respected his wishes."

When her green eyes lifted to his, he stopped dead.

Check out that stare, he thought. So compassionate. So…kind.

As he looked at her face, something popped in his

chest, like a lid being released. And what came out of his inner soda can was a yearning that unsettled him. He literally wanted to dive right into those warm eyes of hers.

"I think the bacon is burning," she said.

He cursed and got back with the program. As he transferred the strips onto a paper towel–covered plate, he asked, "So where are you from?"

"The north shore. Essex. My mother is still up there." Lizzie laughed a little. "I was hoping to introduce your father to her. Maybe they could have been friends. But your father liked to keep to himself."

Or maybe keep *Lizzie* to himself? "You got a husband or a boyfriend there, Lizzie?"

As she blushed again, he became absorbed in the pink tint on her face. To the point that when she dipped her head, he found himself leaning to the side so he could keep measuring her cheeks.

Man, the women he knew in Manhattan did not blush and he realized he liked it. Or hell, maybe he just liked this particular woman turning red.

"Lizzie? Was my question too personal?"

"Not at all. I don't have a husband. Or boyfriend. Too busy."

Good, he thought. Then frowned.

Wait a minute. Not *good*. Doesn't matter. None of his business.

Besides, maybe she'd been saving herself for his *father*. God, what a cringer that was.

"What about you?" she asked. "Are you married?"

"Nope. Not my thing."

"Why not?"

Well, there were a whole bunch of why nots. The first of which was prenups could be broken and he had no intention of someone in stilettos walking off with his hard-earned cash. More than that, though, you had to trust your wife wouldn't play you. And he'd long ago lost the illusion that faith in lovers or business associates could be justified.

Hell, maybe he'd never had it. His two brothers were really the only people on the planet he believed in.

"No particular reason," he said, dumping the eggs into the pan. As a hiss rose up from the hot iron, he tacked on, "Other than I'm a loner."

She smiled. "Like your father."

He whipped his head around. "I am *nothing* like my father."

As she recoiled, he didn't apologize. Some things needed to be stated clearly and he was not like that abusive, drunken bastard on any level.

"You like a lot of pepper in your eggs?" he said to fill up the silence.

Chapter Three

Sean O'Banyon might be a little touchy about his father, but he made a very good breakfast, Lizzie thought, as she put her fork on her clean plate and eased back in the chair.

Wiping her mouth on a paper towel, she glanced across the table. Sean was still eating, but then again he had twice the food she'd taken to get through. And he was slow and meticulous with his meal, which surprised her. He seemed like the kind of tough guy who wouldn't bother with good table manners. But his were beautiful.

And…boy, yeah, the way he ate wasn't the only beautiful thing about him. That chest of his was sinfully good to look at. So were his thick eyelashes. And his mouth—

Lizzie cursed in her head. What was her problem? The man asks her in for breakfast right after his father dies and she's checking him out as if he were an eHarmony candidate?

Then again, it was probably biology talking. After all, when had she last been alone with a man? As she counted up the months, then hit the one-year, then two-year mark, she winced.

Two and a half years ago? How had that happened?

"What's wrong?" Sean asked, obviously catching her expression.

Yeah, like she was going to parade her Death Valley dating life in front of him? "Oh, nothing."

"So what was I about to ask you? Oh…your mother. You said she's still up in Essex?"

"Ah, yes, she is. She's an artist and she loves living by the sea. She keeps busy painting and sketching and trying out just about every kind of creative endeavor you can think of."

To keep her eyes off him, Lizzie folded her paper napkin into a precise square—and thought about her mother's origami period. That year, the Christmas tree had been covered with pointy-headed swans and razor-edged stars. Most of them had been off-kilter, mere approximations of what they were supposed to be, but her mother had adored them, and because of that, Lizzie had loved them, as well.

For no particular reason, she said, "My mother is what they used to call *fey*. Lovely and…"

"All in her head?"

"Precisely."

"So you take care of her, huh? She relies on you for the practical stuff."

As Lizzie flushed, she murmured, "Either you're very perceptive, or I'm quite transparent."

"Little bit of both, I think."

As he smiled, her heart tripped and fell into her gut. Oh…God, he was handsome.

"How long are you in town?" she blurted. And then couldn't believe she'd asked. It wasn't that the question was forward on the surface, but more because she was angling to see him again in a situation just like this. The two of them alone.

Can you say *desperate*, she thought.

"I'm going back to the city tomorrow—well, that's today, isn't it?" He wiped his mouth and took a drink from his glass of orange juice. "But I'll be back. I've got to clean out this place."

"Are you going to sell?"

"No reason to keep it. But I'll make sure you're in the loop."

"Thank you. I really liked living here."

"Hopefully you won't have to leave. I can't believe anyone would want to turn this into a one-family."

"I think I'm going to want to move, though."

"Why?"

She looked around. "It won't be the same without him."

Sean frowned and fell silent so she got up and took both their plates to the sink. As she washed them with a sponge she'd bought a week and a half ago, she tried not to think that Mr. O'Banyon had still been alive back then.

"So you and my father were real tight, huh?"

She held a plate under the rushing water. "We used to watch TV together. And we always ate dinner up here on Sundays. We also looked out for each other. It was nice to think someone wondered whether or not I made it back from my night shifts. Made me feel safer."

And cared for.

With her mother, Lizzie had always been the watcher, the worrier, the keeper…even when she'd been young. For the time she had known Mr. O'Banyon, it had been really nice to be something other than a ghost on the periphery of someone's artistic inspiration.

Feeling awkward, she asked, "So do you live right in Manhattan?"

"Yeah."

"I've always wanted to go there," she murmured as she put the plate in the drying rack. "It seems so exciting and glamorous."

"City's not far from here. Just drive down some time."

She shook her head, thinking of the time she would have to take off from work. "I couldn't really afford to. With two jobs, my hours are long and my mother needs the money more than I need a vacation. Besides, who am I kidding? I'm a homebody at heart."

"And you were happy being a homebody here. With my father."

She picked up a towel and began to dry what she'd washed. "Yes, I was."

"Were you lovers?"

"What?" She nearly dropped the skillet. "Why would you think that?"

His eyes were cold and cynical as he said, "Not unheard-of."

"Maybe to you. We were friends. Good Lord…"

She quickly put away the dishes, hung up the towel and headed for the exit. "Thank you for breakfast."

He rose from the table. "Elizabeth—"

"Lizzie." She stepped around him pointedly. "Just Lizzie."

He took her arm in a firm grip. "I'm sorry if I offended you."

She leveled her stare on his hard face. His apology seemed sincere enough; though his eyes remained remote, they didn't waver from hers and his tone was serious.

She reminded herself that he was under a lot of stress and it was four—well, almost five in the morning. She cleared her throat. "It's all right. This is a hard time for you right now."

"Hard time for you, too, right?"

"Yes," she said in a small voice. "Very. I'm going to miss him."

Sean reached out and touched her cheek, surprising her. "You know something?"

"What?"

"A woman like you should have someone waiting up for her, Lizzie."

In a flash, she became totally aware of him down to the details of his beard's dark shadow and the hazel of his eyes and…

And the fact that he was looking at her mouth.

From out of nowhere, an arc of heat supercharged

the air between their bodies and Lizzie had to part her lips to breathe.

Except just as she did, his face masked over and he dropped her arm. "I'll walk you to the door."

He turned away as if nothing had happened.

Okay…so had she just imagined all that?

Apparently.

Lizzie forced herself to walk out of the kitchen and found him standing next to the apartment's open door. As if she'd overstayed her welcome.

As Sean waited for Lizzie to come from the kitchen, he figured he either needed to put his long-tailed button-down shirt on or get her out of here. Because his body was stating its opinion of her loud and clear, and he didn't want to embarrass the poor woman.

He was totally, visibly aroused. And the quick rear-range he'd done as he'd walked through the living room had only helped so much.

Then things got worse. As she came over, he started to wonder exactly what was under that baggy shirt of hers—and his "problem" got harder.

"Are you going to have a funeral for him?" she asked.

Well, at least that question slapped him back to reality.

"No. He'll be cremated and interred next to my mother. Told me ten years ago he didn't want any kind of memorial service." Man, that had been an ugly phone call. His father had been drunk at the time, naturally, and had maintained he didn't want his three sons dancing on his coffin.

Sean had hung up at that point.

"That's a shame." Lizzie tucked a piece of blond hair behind her ear. "For both of you. People should be remembered. Fathers should be remembered."

As those green eyes met his, they were like looking into a still pond, gentle, calming, warm. Teamed with the heat that had sprung up in his blood, the impact of her compassionate stare was like getting sucker punched: a surprise that numbed him out.

Unease snaked through him. Stripped of defenses and vaguely needy was not what he wanted to be, not around anyone.

His voice grew harsh. "Oh, I'll remember him, all right. Good night, Lizzie."

She quickly looked away and scooted past him. As she hit the stairs at a fast clip, she spoke over her shoulder. "Goodbye, Sean."

Sean shut the door, crossed his arms over his chest and leaned back against the wall. As he thought about his arousal, he reminded himself that there was nothing mystical or unusual at work here. Lizzie was attractive. He was half-naked. They were alone. Do the math.

Except there was something else, wasn't there?

He thought back to the past. Though his memories of his mother were indistinct, he recalled her as warm and kind, the quintessential maternal anchor. From what he'd learned about her, she'd come from a very good family who'd disowned her when she'd married a blue-collar Irish Catholic. Her parents had even refused to come to her memorial service.

Back when she'd still been around, their father had

been relatively stable, but that had changed after she'd died when Sean was five. After they'd buried her, all hell had broken loose and hard drinking had moved into the apartment like a mean houseguest. Turned out Anne had been the glue that had held Eddie together. Without her, he'd spiraled fast, hit bottom hard and never resurfaced.

Sean stared at the Barcalounger.

Dimly, he heard the water come on downstairs and he imagined Lizzie brushing her teeth over a sink. When the whining rush was cut off, he saw her stripping off those jeans and sliding between clean white sheets.

She looked like the kind of woman who had sensible sheets.

She hadn't been his father's lover, he thought. The outrage on her face had been too spontaneous, the offense too quick. But that didn't mean she hadn't been stringing Eddie along for money.

God, one look into those green eyes and even Sean had been hypnotized.

Picturing her face, he was surprised that he wanted to believe she was a well of compassion and goodness. But the Mother Teresa routine was tough to buy. That talk about wanting to go to Manhattan, but needing to hold down two jobs to help out her fey, artistic mother? It was almost Dickensian.

He went back over to the couch and lay down. As he put his arm under his head, a small voice he didn't trust told him he was reading her wrong. He ignored the whisper, chalking it up to the fact that he was off-kilter because he was back in his father's place.

When his cell phone went off at 6:00 a.m., he was

still awake, having watched the sun rise behind the veil of the old lace drapes.

Sitting up, he grabbed his BlackBerry and checked the number. "Billy."

His brother's low voice came through loud and clear. "I was crashed when you called and just woke up for practice. Are you okay—"

"He's dead, Billy." He didn't need to use any better word than *he*. There was only one *him* among the three O'Banyon brothers.

As a long, slow exhale came over the phone, Sean wished he'd told Billy in person.

"When?" Billy asked.

"Last night. Heart attack."

"You call Mac?"

"Yeah. But God knows when he'll get the message."

"Where are you?"

"Home frickin' sweet home."

There was a sharp inhale. "You shouldn't be there. That's not a good place."

Sean looked around and couldn't agree more. "Trust me, I'm leaving as soon as I can."

"Is there anything I—"

"Nah. There's not much to do. Finnegan's will handle the cremation and he'll be interred next to Mom. I'll go back and forth until I've packed everything up here and put the house on the market. I mean, I don't want to keep this place."

"Neither do I. Mac'll agree."

In the long silence that followed, Sean knew he and

his brother were remembering exactly the same kinds of things.

"I'm glad he's gone," Billy finally said.

"Me, too."

After they hung up, Sean felt exhaustion settle on him like a suit of chain mail. Stretching out on the sofa, he closed his lids and gave up fighting the past, letting the memories fill the space behind his eyes. Though he was six foot four and worth about a billion dollars, in the dimness, on this couch, in the apartment that had been a hell for him and his brothers, he was as small as a child and just as powerless.

So he was not at all surprised when two hours later he woke up screaming and covered in sweat. The nightmare, the one he'd had for years, had come for another visit.

Jacking upright, he gasped and rubbed his face. The summer morning was bright and cheerful, the light barging into the living room through the windows like a four-year-old wanting to play.

Amid the lovely sunshine, he felt positively elderly.

In a desperate, misplaced bid to cleanse his mind, he took a shower. Didn't help. No matter how hard he worked his body with soap, he couldn't lose the head spins about the past. It felt as if he were trapped in a car on a closed track, going around and around without getting anywhere.

As he stepped out of the water and toweled off, he knew his best hope was that his mind would run out of gas. Soon.

Man, he couldn't wait to get back to Manhattan tonight.

Chapter Four

Two days later, Lizzie lost her job at the Roxbury Community Heath Initiative.

It was the end of a long Friday and she was in the medical-records room when her boss came to find her. "Lizzie? You have a minute?"

She glanced up from the patient charts she was pulling. Dr. Denisha Roberts, the clinic's director, was in the doorway looking exhausted. Which made sense. It was almost five in the afternoon and it had been a week full of challenges. As usual, finances were very tight and their waiting room busier than ever.

Lizzie frowned. "What's wrong?"

"Can you come down to my office?"

Lizzie hugged the chart in her hands against her

chest and followed Denisha to the back of the clinic. After they'd gone into the office and Lizzie was in a chair, the director took a deep breath, then shut the door.

"I don't know how to say this so I'm just going to come right out with it." Denisha sat on the edge of her desk, her dark eyes somber. "I've been informed that our funding from the state is going to be cut substantially for the upcoming year."

"Oh, no…don't tell me we're closing. The community needs us."

"We'll have enough to stay open and I'm going to put some grant applications out there, which hopefully will generate some funds. But…I need to make some staffing changes."

Lizzie closed her eyes. "Let me guess, first in, first out."

"I'm so sorry, Lizzie. You make a tremendous contribution here, you really do, and I'm going to give you my highest recommendation. It's just that with everyone else doing such a good job, seniority is the only thing I can base the choice on. And I have to make the cut now, before the funding shrinks, because we need that new X-ray machine."

Lizzie smoothed her hand over the patient file in her arms. She knew exactly the person it detailed. Sixty-eight-year-old Adella Thomas, a grandmother of nine, who had bad asthma and a gospel voice that could charm the birds to the trees. Whenever one of Adella's granddaughters brought her in for her checkups, she always sang for the staff as well as the patients in the waiting room.

"When's my last day?" Lizzie asked.

"The end of this month. Labor Day weekend. And we'll give you a month's severance." There was a hesitation. "We're in real trouble, Lizzie. Please understand…this is killing me."

She thought for a moment. "You know…I can line up moonlighting work easily enough. Why don't we say a week from today so you can get me off the books? I'll still have a month after that to find a day job."

"That would be…the best thing you could do for us." Denisha looked down at her hands then twisted her wedding band around and around. "I hate doing this. You can't know how much we'll miss you."

"Maybe I can still volunteer."

Denisha nodded her head sadly. "We'd love to have you. Any way we can."

When Lizzie left the office a little later, she thought she was likely losing the best boss she'd ever have. Dr. Roberts had that rare combination of compassion and practicality that worked so well in medicine. She was also an inspiration, giving so much back to the community she'd grown up in. The joke around the center was that she should run for governor someday.

Except the staff really meant it.

Lizzie walked down to the medical-records room and finished pulling charts so that the Saturday-morning staff would be ready for their first five patients of the day. Then she grabbed her lunch tote from the kitchen, waved goodbye to the other nurses and headed out into the oven that was your typical early August evening in Boston.

On her way home, she called Boston Medical Center and asked her supervisor to put her on the sub list so she could hopefully log more hours in the ED. She would need a financial cushion if she couldn't find another day job right away and she might as well prepare for the worst.

When she pulled up to the duplex, she told herself it was going to be fine. She had an excellent job history, and with the number of hospitals in and around Boston, she would secure another position in a week or two.

But God…wherever she ended up it wasn't going to be as special as the clinic. There was just something about that place, probably because it was run more like an old-fashioned doctor's office than a modern-day, insurance-driven, patient-churning business.

Lizzie's mood lifted long enough for her to get through her front door, but the revival didn't last as she hit the message button on her answering machine. Her mother's voice, that singsong, perpetually cheerful, girlie rush, was like the chatter of a goldfinch.

Funny how draining such a pretty sound could be.

"Hi-ho, Lizzie-fish, I just *had* to call you because I've been looking at kilns today for my pottery, which is *critical* for my new direction in my work, which as you know has recently been drifting *away* from painting and into things of a more three-dimensional nature, which is really *significant* for my growth as an artist, which is…"

Lizzie's mom used the word *which* as most people did a period.

As the message went on and on, Lizzie put her purse

and her keys down and leafed through the mail. Bill. Bill. Flyer. Bill.

"Anyway, Lizzie-fish, I bought one this morning and it's being delivered tomorrow. The credit card was broken so I wrote the check for two thousand dollars and I had to pay more for Saturday delivery…."

Lizzie froze. Then whipped her head around to stare at the machine. Two thousand dollars? *Two thousand dollars?* There wasn't that kind of cash in their joint account. And it was after five so Lizzie couldn't call the local bank to stop payment.

Her mother had just bounced that check good and hard.

Lizzie cut off the message and deleted it, then sat down in the quilt-covered armchair by the front bay windows.

The credit card was not "broken." Lizzie had put a five-hundred-dollar limit on the thing precisely so her mother couldn't charge things like kilns, for God's sake.

At least this situation was repairable, though. First thing tomorrow morning, she'd call the bank and cancel that check, then she'd get in touch with the one art-supply store in Essex and tell them the purchase was off. Hopefully, she'd catch them in time.

A thump drifting down from above jerked Lizzie to attention. She looked at the ceiling then out the window. Another rental car was parked at the curb, this time a silver one, but she'd been too caught up in the drama over her job to notice when she'd arrived.

Sean O'Banyon was back.

Sean stood in his old bedroom and wondered how many boxes he'd need to clean out the space. On his way into Southie from the airport, he'd hit U-Haul and bought two dozen of their cardboard specials, but he was probably going to need more.

He went over and opened up the closet door then tugged on a white string that had a little metal crown at the end. The light clicked on and the dusty remnants of his and Billy's high-school wardrobe were revealed. The two of them had shared clothes for years because Billy had always been so big for his age, and when Sean had left for college, they'd divvied up the best of the stuff. All that was left now was a wilted chamois shirt with a hole under one pit and a pair of khakis they'd both hated.

His cell phone rang and he answered it offhandedly, distracted by thoughts of his brother. It was the team of analysts from his office about the Condi-Foods merger, and he started to pace around as he answered their questions.

When he got off the phone with them, he looked back across the room at the closet and frowned. There was something shoved in the far corner of the upper shelf, something he'd missed on the booze hunt that first night he'd been here.

A backpack. His backpack.

He went over, stretched up and grabbed on to a pair of nylon straps. Whatever was in the damn thing weighed a ton, and as it swung loose from the shelf, he let it fall to the floor. As it landed, a little cloud of dust wafted up and dispersed.

Crouching down, he unzipped the top and his breath

caught. Books… His books. The ones from his senior year in high school.

He took out his old physics tome, first smoothing his palm over the cover then fingering the gouge he'd made on the spine. Cracking the thing open, he put his nose into the crease and breathed in deep, smelling the sweet scent of ink on bound pages. After tracing over notes he'd made in the margins, he put it aside.

Good Lord, his calculus book. His AP chemistry. His AP history.

As he spread them out flat on the floor and arranged them so the tops of their multicolored covers were aligned, he had a familiar feeling, one he used to get in school. Looking at them he felt rich. Positively rich. In a childhood full of hand-me-downs and birthdays with no parties and Christmases with no presents, learning had been his luxury. His happiness. His wealth.

After countless petty thefts as a juvenile delinquent, these textbooks had been the last things he'd stolen. When the end of his senior school year had come, he just hadn't been able to give them back and he hadn't had the money to pay for them. So he'd marked each one of the spines and turned them in as you were supposed to. Then he'd broken into the school and the gouges he'd made had been how he'd found the ones that were his. He'd gathered them from the various stacks, put them in this backpack and raced away into the night.

Of course he'd felt guilty as hell. Strange that palming booze from convenience stores had never bothered his conscience, but he'd felt that the taking of the books had been wrong. So as soon as he'd earned enough from his campus job at Harvard, he'd sent the high school three hundred seventy-five dollars in cash with an anonymous note explaining what it was for.

But he'd needed to have the books. He'd needed to know they were still with him as he went off to Harvard. On some irrational level, he'd feared if he didn't keep them, everything he'd learned from them would disappear, and he'd been terrified about going to Crimson and looking stupid.

Yeah, *terrified* was the right word. He could clearly recall the day he'd left to go to college...could remember every detail about getting on the T that late August afternoon and heading over the Charles River to Harvard. Unlike a lot of the other guys in his class, who'd come with trunks of clothes and fancy stereos and TVs and refrigerators—and BMWs for God's sake—he'd had nothing but a beat-up suitcase and a duffel bag with a broken strap.

He'd gone alone because he hadn't wanted his father to take him, not that Eddie had offered. And as he'd been forced to go on foot, he'd had to leave his books behind. There had been no question that he was coming back for them, though. He'd returned home that weekend to get the backpack...except his father had said he'd thrown it out.

That had been the last time Sean had been home. Until three nights ago.

A knock brought his head up. Getting to his feet, he walked down the hall to the living room, opened the door and—oh, man—looked into the very pair of green eyes that had been in the back of his mind over the past few days.

Lizzie Bond was dressed in a little white T-shirt and a pair of khaki shorts. Her hair was down on her shoulders, all naturally streaked with blond and brown, and there wasn't a lick of makeup on her pretty face.

She looked fantastic.

"Hi," he said with a slow smile.

In characteristic fashion she flushed. "Hi. I'm…ah, I'm sorry to bother you." She held out a clear plastic bag full of clothes. "I meant to give this to you before. They're your father's things."

He didn't want whatever was in there, but he took the thing anyway. "Thanks."

She glanced around his shoulder at the stack of collapsed U-Haul boxes. "So you're starting the packing."

"No reason to wait." He stepped back and motioned her in. "Listen, if you want any of the stuff around here, you know, the furniture or anything, it's yours."

"Won't you want to keep some?"

"My place is furnished." Sean shut the door to keep the air-conditioning from leaking down the stairwell. And also because he wanted her to stay for a little longer. "So is my brother's."

Her brows shot up. "You have a brother?"

"He didn't mention that?"

"No, he only told me to call you."

Well, hadn't he won the lottery. "There are three of us, actually. Billy, Mac and me. I'm in the middle. Billy's the youngest."

"Oh." She tucked some hair behind her ear, something he had a feeling she did when she felt awkward. "I had no idea. Where are the other two?"

"Here and there." Or in the case of Mac, God only knew where. Matter of fact, he still hadn't returned Sean's call. "Seriously, Lizzie, check out the furniture, tell me what you want and I'll help you move it downstairs. Except for the couch, at least for the time being. I'm going to be sleeping on it until I'm through here."

She gave him an odd look, as if she was thinking there were plenty of beds in the place and was wondering why he didn't use them. But she didn't make any comment, just walked around the living room then headed for the kitchen.

As she wandered around assessing furniture, he found himself wishing he could take the offer back. For some reason, he didn't want this stuff in her home…as if what had taken place here could contaminate where she lived. Which was ridiculous. Domestic abuse wasn't a virus. And sure as hell if it was, you couldn't pick it up from a ratty Barcalounger.

When she went into his and Billy's bedroom, Sean followed, his eyes locking on the sway of her hips as she walked. He let his gaze wander up her spine to her shoulders and her neck. With a flash of inspiration, he wanted to pull her up against him, draw his fingers in deep through her hair, tilt her head back—

"Look at the books!" She crouched down. "These are from high school, right? Were they yours?"

Sean quickly knelt and started stuffing the things into the pack. "They're nothing. Nothing special."

She sat back and he knew she was watching his

frantic hands, but he couldn't stop himself. He'd always had to protect his books and evidently the compulsion hadn't lessened with age. When they were all safely zipped in the bag, he hefted them back onto the shelf in the closet and shut the door.

"So the furniture?" he prompted with an edge. "You want any?"

She got up slowly. "I think not. Thank you."

As she turned away, he knew she was hightailing it for the exit and he didn't blame her. Goddamn it, he'd all but bitten her head off.

"Lizzie?"

She paused in the bedroom doorway, but didn't look at him. "Yes?"

"If I promise to be more polite, would you like to go out for some dinner?"

When her head swiveled around, her eyes were grave. "You don't like it here, do you?"

For some stupid reason, he found himself shaking his head. "I'd rather be just about anywhere else in the world."

"Why?"

"No reason."

The lie was no doubt painfully apparent, yet he was sticking with it. Some things you never shared. Not because you were weak, but because you were strong.

Lizzie stared at Sean and idly thought he looked better than any man should. The black T-shirt and low-hanging jeans were just too attractive. And the fact that he was barefoot was really sexy. Even his feet were nice.

In the silence between them, she was reminded keenly of his father. No matter what Sean said, he and Mr. O'Banyon were a lot alike. Very private. Very closed.

Though she had known Mr. O'Banyon for quite a while, there had been so many things the man had hidden, just as Sean was doing now. And the two of them did it the same way. Their faces just walled up tight, their eyes going blank, their mouths drawing into a line.

"So what do you think?" Sean prompted. "Dinner?"

The thing was, the shutdown happened fast. Literally in a moment, they were gone and you were talking to a two-dimensional likeness of who they really were.

It made her want to dig to find out what had happened in this apartment, what had caused a father and son to split so irrevocably.

Son? *Sons,* she corrected herself. She couldn't believe Mr. O'Banyon hadn't mentioned he had multiple children.

"I'll get my purse," she said, heading for the living room.

"How about Little Italy?" Sean said as he followed.

"Sounds like heaven."

She waited as he shoved his feet into a pair of Nikes, grabbed keys from the table next to the couch and slipped a black wallet into his back pocket.

After a quick stop by her place, they got into his rental. As they pulled away from the curb, she noticed that the tension in his face had eased up considerably and she had a feeling it was because they were leaving.

"Sean?"

"Yeah?"

"About the furniture upstairs? Come to think of it, I could really use that kitchen table and those chairs."

"No problem. When we get back, I'll hump them down to your place."

"That would be great."

She and Mr. O'Banyon had never sat in the kitchen during their Sunday dinners so she didn't have any deep associations with the little dining set. And she needed one. She was tired of eating either standing up in the kitchen with her butt against the counter or off her lap on her couch.

And maybe there was a little part of her that wanted to keep something of Mr. O'Banyon's. As she'd looked at all those boxes Sean was going to use, she'd felt an odd fear…as if her friend were truly disappearing even though he was already gone.

A half hour later she and Sean were standing in line outside Bastianelli's. The restaurant was a Little Italy favorite, barely bigger than a closet with the best Italian food in town. Part of the tradition of eating there was the long line and she always enjoyed the forced slowdown. With nothing to do but inch forward toward the glossy black and brass door, Lizzie found herself calming out and forgetting about the fact that a dear friend had died and she'd lost one of her jobs and her mother was the Imelda Marcos of art supplies.

As the sun set, the heat rolling over the city eased up and a gentle breeze suffused with the scents of oregano and garlic wafted by. The patter of talk from other people in line was like soft, indistinct music, more rhythm than words.

Lizzie lifted her face to the gloaming sky and took a deep breath. When she felt something touch her neck, she jumped.

Sean's hand hesitated then brushed behind her ear. "Loose strand of hair."

In slow motion, his fingers drifted over to the other side of her face and did the same thing. "And another one."

Abruptly, she couldn't breathe at all. Which was fine. Looking up into his hazel eyes, she didn't need air to live.

His thumb passed over her cheek and his voice dropped an octave, becoming nothing more than a deep rumble in that muscled chest of his. "You've got bruises under your eyes from lack of sleep. What's got you so tired there, Lizzie?"

She blinked. Then wanted to wince because obviously he thought she looked like hell. "Just have a lot on my mind."

"Like what?" he said in a lazy drawl.

Oh, God…where to go with that one? Because the truth was that she'd stayed awake thinking of him. "I'm out of work," she blurted.

All at once, his voice shifted back to its normal bass and he dropped his hand. "What happened?"

Way to ruin a moment, Lizzie.

She cleared her throat. "Well, the health clinic in Roxbury where I work is losing state funding so they have to reduce staff. We're just a small community center and we don't—*they*…don't have enough resources to afford my position anymore."

His brows came together. "This because of the new budget?"

"Yes. Tax dollars are tight and I can understand that. But the state has to support facilities like ours. I mean…theirs." She exhaled in a rush. "It's a social imperative."

As they moved forward again, she realized there was one more couple and then they'd be in the door and at a table.

She looked through the restaurant's window at the people who were eating inside and murmured, "I'm going to miss working at the clinic so much. The patients are wonderful and I've really gotten to know the community. But I'm going to volunteer there or at least try to."

"How long do you have until you're out?"

"Next Friday. But I'm sure I'll find more work. Nurses are always needed in Boston. Besides, I still have my moonlighting. I'll be fine." When there was a silence, she glanced over at him. "Why are you looking at me like that?"

"Like what?"

"As if you're measuring me."

Sean's lids dropped and a slow, very masculine smile appeared on his face. "Well, you're kind of measurable, Lizzie Bond."

Whoa.

Flustered, she said, "It's hot out here."

"Yeah, it is."

And didn't that drawl of his just make it hotter?

Abruptly, he laughed. "You are a blusher."

"Not usually."

"Well, then I appreciate your making the effort on my behalf. It suits you."

Oh…hell. She had to smile at him. Just couldn't resist looking up into those deep-set hazel eyes and grinning like a fool.

The door to Bastianelli's opened and a little man with a mustache and a big belly motioned them in with a broad smile. As they stepped into the restaurant, Sean put his hand on the small of her back and she found herself inching closer to his body.

And not because the place was crowded.

As they made their way to the table, Sean leaned down to her ear, the spicy scent of his cologne enveloping her like a caress. "You've surprised me."

"I have?" God, even though they were in a public place, she suddenly felt as though they were all alone. And she liked it.

His chest brushed up against her shoulder blades. "I didn't know I liked women who blushed. Also didn't know I liked Ivory soap so much."

"How did you know I used…"

Her words dried up as his fingertip ran down the nape of her neck. "I can smell it on you."

Okay, so now *hot* didn't cover it. She was inside of a volcano.

The maître d' stopped by a little table in the corner that had a red candle burning and two place settings on it. "For you! *Mange bene!*"

As she and Sean sat down, she fumbled with her napkin, aware that she was blushing a little. And that he was looking.

"So how do you feel about red?" he asked, flipping open the wine list.

"Perfect." She was getting to know the color ever so much better with him around.

"Do you want to pick?"

"No, thanks." She took a look at her menu and didn't see a thing. Surely she wasn't reading into things with him. He'd caressed her neck, for heaven's sake. "I'll trust your choice."

"Lizzie?" When she glanced up, he smiled and said softly, "Just wanted to see the blush. That's all."

As her cheeks flamed even further, the waiter came over with some fantastic fresh bread and a plate of olive oil. After the specials were recited, Sean ordered a bottle of wine and they made their selections.

When they were alone, he offered the basket of bread to her. "You know…really, this candlelight suits you."

It was right then that Lizzie knew for sure…she was on a date.

Chapter Five

An hour and a half later, Sean smiled to himself as he put his espresso back down on its little saucer. He couldn't remember when he'd had a more enjoyable dinner with a woman. He and Lizzie had talked about books and movies and food and music.

And they didn't agree on anything. Which was the fun part.

"I can't believe you don't like any of the Impressionists," Lizzie said, shaking her head over her cannoli.

"Oh, please." He smiled more widely. "Rorschach tests and finger painting do more for me."

"So what kind of art do you like?"

He forked up a little more of his crème caramel. "Medieval. Definitely medieval."

"Really?"

He laughed. "Why so surprised?"

"It's not what I expected."

"And what exactly would you expect? Edward Hopper? No, wait, LeRoy Neiman?"

She sipped some of her cappuccino. "Well, I, ah...I'm just surprised you care about art at all. Or know so much about it." She rushed to qualify. "Not that I think you're uncultured or anything. It's just..."

He leaned back in his chair, feeling a little awkward for the first time. "Just that considering where I come from, men aren't usually into that stuff?"

She winced. "That sounds bad doesn't it? I don't mean to offend you or generalize."

"Nah, it's okay. Beautiful things should be valued, so I like art. No big deal."

The awkward feeling persisted. Thing was, he liked that she thought he was just another Joe from Southie, that she seemed to have no clue who he was. He'd been Sean O'Banyon, Big Shot Wall Street Money Man, for so long, it felt liberating to leave that identity behind.

And just be himself.

Except he was leaving a hell of a lot out and that didn't sit well.

She took another bite of the cannoli and wiped her mouth. "You know a lot more about literature than I would have thought, too."

"Always been a big reader."

She smiled and he loved the curve of her cheeks in the candlelight. "So tell me, what do you do? I've been meaning to ask you."

The waiter showed up at Sean's elbow. "Another espresso? More cappuccino?"

"Not for me, thanks. Lizzie? No? Okay, the check would be great."

The waiter left and Sean folded his napkin and put it on the table. God, how to answer her. This had been the best date he'd been on in…forever. All it had been was two people getting to know each other and he didn't want to ruin it.

Especially because he didn't know for a fact that she hadn't been using his father for money.

Except, damn it, Lizzie just did not seem like that kind of woman.

Sean cursed in his head. Yeah, well, neither had the one who had taken him for such a ride way back when.

"My work?" He shrugged…and recalled the conversation he'd had with his team before he and Lizzie had gone out. Nothing but interest-rate analysis and speculation on whether the Fed was going to raise the rates in the next quarter. Dry. Very dry. "You know what, it's not that interesting, I'm afraid."

"Are you in construction?"

His brows shot up. "What makes you think that?"

As Lizzie turned bright pink again, he wanted to lean across their empty cups and kiss her. So much so, he planted his palms on the table and started to rise.

But come on. Trying to do that for the first time in public? Not smooth.

As he forced himself back into the chair, he knew he was going to end up putting a move on her at the end of the night. He *knew* it. It was probably a bad idea but she was so different...so natural...so real. A woman, not a social shark in a skirt.

Or at least she appeared that way.

"Why do you think I'm in construction, Lizzie?"

"Your chest is really...ah...developed. So I thought maybe what you did had a physical component to it." Then she frowned and looked down. "Except your hands aren't callused. Are you a trainer at a gym?"

"I do train folks, yeah." And this was not a lie. He worked a lot with the membership of his triathlon club, getting folks ready for events. "I'm into sports."

"What kinds?"

"Every year I do the Ironman Triathlon. I hit a number of others, but that's my big one. I like to compete. And I like to win."

"You like to push yourself, then."

"Yeah, I do. So do my brothers. We're like that."

"Why?"

The question made warning bells go off in his head. He and Billy and Mac were all driven to the point of obsession and the root cause, he suspected, was in the ugly past: every day, they ran without running.

Time to switch the subject.

Sean shrugged. "We're just like that. So tell me more about your mom. What kind of art is she into?"

God, he was a liar, wasn't he?

And she knew it. Her smart, level eyes told him that.

Lizzie smiled at him, and it was the smile of a Madonna, all-knowing, very kind. "It's okay, Sean. I'm not going to push."

Crap. Now he was the one flushing. Imagine that. "I'm not into talking about myself much."

"That's all right. You're really good company anyway."

Sean's heart stopped. He couldn't think of the last time a woman had told him he was really good company. Hell, maybe one never had. And he was so used to being seen as a "catch" that the idea someone just liked his words and his opinions was…disarming.

"You're some good company there, too, Lizzie." His voice was a little husky and he hoped she didn't notice it. He cleared his throat. "I am curious about your mom, though. What's she like?"

Lizzie took a deep breath, as if she were about to lift something heavy off the floor. "My mother calls herself a free-range art-ellectual. I'm not too clear on what exactly that is, but I can tell you that she's into pottery now. I don't think it's going to stick. Over the past two decades, she's been through almost everything. Painting in watercolor and oil. Sculpting in clay, marble and brass. Pastels. Photography. Macramé. Toothpicks. Recycle art—that's garbage by the way. She follows her whims where they take her."

"She sell any of her work in galleries?"

"She's more into the creation end of things rather than the retail." Lizzie sipped at her cappuccino. "And well…honestly? She's not that good at it."

"Sounds like an expensive hobby then."

Lizzie's voice grew wry. "Yeah. But the thing is, it makes her happy. So I support it."

"Where's your father?"

"He left about five years ago for the third time and

it finally stuck. My mother is enchanting, but she can be difficult to handle. She's a child in many ways, and like a child, she's both irresponsible and beguiling. So I can't say I blame him."

"Do you see him?"

She shook her head. "When he left, he left us both. Said a clean cut was best. It was no big change, though. She was always what held his interest, not me."

Good Lord, he thought. "That's harsh."

"Oh, I don't mean to come across that way."

"Not you, Lizzie. Him. To leave his daughter like that?"

There was a quiet moment. Then she murmured, "I think it's hard for him to see me. I look a lot like her and our voices sound the same. To him, I am the younger version of her."

"So what? He should man up and get over that."

Her eyes flipped to his, and as he saw the sadness in them, he wanted to hunt down her father and yell at the guy for dumping his daughter.

The urge got even stronger when she said with dignity, "It is what it is. I used to hope he'd be different, but he is who he is and it's better for me…healthier…to accept him and move on. Waiting for change is hard and not all that realistic."

Yeah, well, Sean respected the fact that she wasn't looking for sympathy and he could see her point, but it still sucked. "You don't have any brothers or sisters do you?"

"No."

"Which means you deal with your mom all by yourself."

"Yes, but it's not that bad. The house is paid for and her expenses aren't that high. Usually."

He kept his curse to himself. "No offense, but it strikes me that the parent-child thing is ass-backward."

"But I love my mother. And without me…"

"She'd be forced to grow up?" In the silence that followed, Sean cursed out loud. "I'm sorry. I don't mean to get in your face about this."

There was another long pause. Then she said, "I don't tell people this usually, not because I'm ashamed or embarrassed, but because I'm not interested in pity…. My mom's mentally challenged. She can function independently to a point, but she's always going to need help. First my father was that for her. Now I am."

Sean's eyes widened. "Oh, God…Lizzie, I'm sorry."

"Don't be." She smiled. "There is no tragedy here and no shame, either. You know, it's interesting. My father is much older than my mom and I assume in the beginning he thought that she was just young and eccentric. Like she'd grow out of her ways or something. It wasn't until I was in my early teens that he took her to doctors and we learned that it was not an issue of maturity. But again, there is no catastrophe here. My mother's happy and healthy and she's full of joy. So it's okay. But can you understand why things between her and I aren't just a case of a parent dropping the ball?"

"Yeah. Totally."

The waiter showed up with the check, and without even thinking, Sean took out his wallet.

"How much do I owe?" Lizzie asked.

Sean froze. He'd been about to pay the whole thing and to hell with his Dutch rule.

Get back with the program, he told himself. Stay tight.

Doing some quick division in his head, he said, "Sixty-seven dollars."

Her eyes flared, but she reached for her purse.

"Let me pay for the wine, though," he cut in. "I picked it."

"No, that's okay. I drank my share."

As she put three twenties, one five and two ones on the table, he noticed that the edges of her purse were worn through. In a rush, his net worth funneled into his brain, that cool billion dollars or so in stocks and cash and annuities and T-bills and gold.

He reached out to push her money back to her.

"Wow, that's a beautiful wallet you have."

He stopped, jarred as his normal mind-set about women returned.

Man, that stuff about Lizzie losing her job had seemed true enough and so had all those blushes and the revelation about her mother. But he got tangled whenever he thought about her relationship with his father. Surely she couldn't have enjoyed that miserable bastard's company. So that left Good Samaritan-itis. Or her being after something.

Sean looked into her eyes and mined for the answer to his unspoken question: Was Lizzie Bond different than the women he knew or exactly the same?

After a moment, he found himself slowly moving her money back toward her. "My treat."

"Are you sure?"

"Yeah." Keeping his titanium American Express card out of sight, he put a crisp hundred-dollar bill and three twenties on top of the table. "Let's go."

"Wow, that's a big tip."

"They deserve it."

She smiled at him. Then stood up…only to put her hand on the wall to steady herself. "Oh, this is bad."

"What?"

"That wine was awfully good and I have no tolerance whatsoever."

"Lean on me, then."

As he came around and drew her against him, their bodies fit together so perfectly it momentarily stopped him in his tracks.

"Sean? You ready to go?"

He tightened his hold on her waist. "Yeah."

He led her through the crowded restaurant, and as he urged her out the door first, he wanted to keep his arm around her. Like for the rest of the night.

When they were outside, she took a couple of deep inhales and said, "Maybe it was just hot in there."

"It was stuffy. You feel better?"

"Much." She glanced to the sky. "I heard we're supposed to get storms tonight."

"Hot enough for it."

"Yes."

He had no idea what they were talking about. Maybe the weather? Whatever. He was caught up in her profile, most specifically her lips. Oh, man…he wanted to grab her around the waist, get her against him from shoulder to knee and kiss the ever-living breath out of her.

"The car's this way," he said roughly.

On the way back to Southie, they went without air-conditioning and both put their windows down. The summer night was gentle and warm as it flooded into the rental car and he stole glances across the seat at her as if he were sixteen.

When they pulled up to the row house, he stopped the sedan and turned off the engine, but he made no move to open his door.

"Thank you," she said with a smile that melted him. "This was lovely."

"You're welcome."

In the silence, he thought of the last time he'd taken a woman out in Manhattan. The two of them had gone to Jean Georges in his limo. She'd been wearing diamond studs the size of marbles and a dress by Chanel; he'd been in one of his Savile Row suits. They'd worked the crowd on the way to their A-lister table then flirted as sophisticates did, one-upping each other. Afterward, they'd gone back to his penthouse, but she hadn't spent the whole night—yet another of his rules with women.

It had all been very glamorous…and utterly forgettable.

Tonight with Lizzie was not. Here in this Ford Taurus, with the summer air on his face and the sound of crickets in his ears and the dark night wrapped around them, this moment was totally vivid to him. He was not on social autopilot. With Lizzie…he was alive.

And he wanted more. He wanted the privacy of her

apartment. He wanted to be in between her sheets. Tonight, he craved the sweetness in her, needed to be naked against her kindness. And though he was very aware that he couldn't give anything back to her other than pleasure, he vowed to make sure that was enough for her if she let him in.

He pushed his door open. "Let's move that kitchen table down."

"Are you sure?" She smiled as they went up onto the porch. "It's late. We could do it tomorrow as I'm off."

"Won't take long. Besides, it'll give me some room for the boxes."

"Oh, in that case, let's do it."

They went upstairs, and as she headed into the kitchen, he walked over to his duffel bag of clothes and took out his shaving kit. As he slipped a condom in his back pocket, he didn't like the ache in his chest, but he didn't stop himself. After all, if she told him no, he would absolutely back off.

"Sean? You coming?" she called out.

"Yeah." He rubbed his sternum and went into the kitchen.

"This is going to be a tight squeeze." She bent to the side and eyed the table's girth. "The stairs aren't that wide."

"Don't worry, we'll take it slow."

Getting the thing down the stairwell took some maneuvering, but they managed not to mash anyone's fingers on the railing or the doorjamb into her apartment.

As they took a breather in her living room, his chest burned even more as he looked around. Everything was tidy and very clean, but thrift-shop worn: the couch had a pretty flowered blanket tucked into what undoubtedly were frayed cushions. The chair by the window had threadbare patches on the arms and was covered by a quilt. There was no TV and just one lamp. Nothing on the walls.

He thought of her purse with its worn corners.

"Sean?"

"I'm sorry, what?"

"Only a little farther." She nodded over her shoulder. "To my kitchen?"

"Right." He picked up his end of the table.

The kitchen was likewise sparkling from regular cleaning—hell, you could have eaten off the floor or the counters. But there was nothing around, no decorations, no extra appliances. Just the basics.

He thought of his own kitchen back in Manhattan with its Viking stove and its granite countertops and its wine fridge and its matching toaster and mixer and espresso machines. None of which he'd ever used.

"Would you like to wait to do the chairs?" she prompted, making him realize he'd been standing stock-still and saying nothing.

"Nah, let's do them now."

Two joint trips up and down and everything was set up in the middle of her kitchen. As Lizzie eased one of the chairs into the table, her hands lingered on its back. The furniture was well used, but she treated it as if it were precious.

"Thank you," she said. "I've always eaten on the couch. Now I have a real table."

Sean rubbed his chest again. How she shamed him with her pleasure at this gift that meant nothing to him.

"You're welcome," he replied, aware he'd made up his mind. "Good night, Lizzie. Sleep well."

As he headed out of the kitchen, he glanced down the hall and saw into one of the bedrooms. It was empty, just four walls and a bare floor. He was willing to bet she only had a bed for herself.

He walked even faster toward the exit.

"Sean?"

He paused with his hand on the door and didn't look back. "Yeah?"

As she hesitated, he guessed she was surprised he wasn't putting a move on her.

"Ah...thank you again for dinner. That was very generous."

Generous? The night before, he'd spent seventeen hundred dollars hosting two people at the Congress Club in Manhattan. But sure as hell, he'd enjoyed the dinner with her in Little Italy so much more.

She cleared her throat. "Maybe I can pay you back sometime."

Now he glanced over his shoulder at her. Standing across the room from him, she was lovely in the way of a summer afternoon. Warm. Inviting. Something you missed during winter.

"Don't worry about it," he said and turned away.

As he closed the door behind himself, he knew if she'd been any other woman he would have stayed. But Lizzie Bond deserved better than a quick roll. And that was all he had in him.

Chapter Six

Lizzie watched Sean walk out her door and wondered yet again if she hadn't read him wrong. She'd been convinced he was going to kiss her, especially after he'd put his arm around her while they'd left the restaurant. She'd even figured that moving the table was just an excuse for him to come into her apartment.

But maybe she'd let her own attraction to him color her interpretation of his actions.

She sucked at dating. Or whatever tonight was.

As she locked her door, she listened to his heavy footsteps going up the stairs and then moving around above her. All things considered, it was probably better for the night to end like this. She could see herself getting attached to him and getting hurt.

It still was a letdown though.

Unsettled and vaguely depressed, she took a quick shower, turned the temperature to low on the AC unit and got into bed.

The lightning came hours later, flashing on the other side of the Venetian blinds, startling her out of sleep. As her heart rate slowed, she listened for the thunder, and after a long pause, a crack dissolved into a bass rumble.

She reached for the remote to the AC and shut the thing off so she could hear better. She'd always loved storms, especially the—

What was that?

She frowned and looked at the ceiling. An odd noise was coming from upstairs, some kind of... Well, she didn't know what that was. She sat up, as if that would help her ears do their job, and held her breath.

There it was again. A low, uneven sound.

Slipping from bed, she walked out into her living room and got really quiet as she absorbed the sounds in the duplex.

Whatever it had been seemed to have stopped.

Except then the next burst of lightning came, and in the dead space before the thunder, she heard what had to be a moan. She opened her door, stepped into the foyer, and put her hand on the staircase's railing. When the low, aching groan came once more, she jogged up and knocked.

"Sean?"

Thunder rolled through the house like a wrecking ball, making the walls vibrate and the darkness of the stairwell seem horror-movie oppressive. Then a hoarse yell came through the door.

She tossed out all propriety and tried the knob. As it was unlocked, she shoved hard and burst into the apartment.

Sean was on the couch, his big body contorted, his boxers twisted around his hips, one arm rigid and gripping a cushion. His head was thrown back, his neck straining, his mouth open as he breathed in ragged pulls. Next to him on the floor was the backpack full of books.

She rushed over and put her hand on his shoulder. "Sean…wake up."

He shot out of the nightmare like a bullet from a gun, sitting up in a rush, shouting loudly. As he swiveled his head toward her, his eyes were stark wild and the moment he saw her, he cowered back, lifting both arms to cover his head as if she were going to strike him.

"No…" His voice didn't sound at all like the one she knew. "No, *please*."

"Sean?" She touched his thick bicep only to have him flinch away and tremble as lightning flickered through the room.

Another crack of thunder broke out, so loud it was as if the house next door had been struck. Both of them jumped. Then Sean dropped his arms and looked around as if he wasn't sure what had happened.

"You had a nightmare."

His eyes went to her face and locked on her as if he were using the sight of her to pull himself out of where he'd been. As he stared up at her, he was breathing hard, the sheen of sweat on his bare chest catching the reflection of yet more bolts of lightning.

He moved so fast, she couldn't have pulled back if she'd wanted to. His hands clamped on either side of her face and he brought her down hard to his mouth.

He kissed her with erotic aggression, the pent-up energy in his body tunneling into her and lighting her on fire through the shifting contact of their mouths. As she gasped, his tongue shot into her mouth and he pulled her on top of him until she felt him from her collarbones to her ankles. Moving fast and hot, he devoured her, holding her with heavy hands, thrusting his hips up into her so she felt his erection.

When he pulled back, they were both panting.

"Leave now," he said roughly. "If you're going to."

She should go, she really should. She'd never been with someone outside of a relationship, and she and Sean definitely didn't have one of those.

Except this moment, this raw, incendiary moment, was too enticing to walk away from.

Sean lowered his hands and held out his arms as if wanting to make sure he wasn't forcing her in any way. "Lizzie, make up your mind. And do it now."

She shook her head. "I don't want to go. I'm not going to stop this—"

He was all over her in the next heartbeat, kissing her like a man possessed, like a man who was starving. His mouth and tongue devastated her, and in the back of her mind, she had some dim thought that he was very good at this, had no doubt had a lot of practice.

Her heart ached at the passing realization, but the

sting didn't linger. She refused to let it. She had him here and now and he was…on fire.

His thigh pushed between hers and his need rubbed on her lower belly, a stunning length that left her shivering. As the storm swept in and the rain came down, he stripped off her shirt and pulled her up his body so he could take one of her breasts into his mouth.

She cried out and arched her back, feeling his hands grab on to the backs of her thighs and squeeze. It was impossible to keep up with him and unthinkable to slow him down and unbearable to imagine him ever stopping. Somehow her panties disappeared, probably because he ripped the side apart.

And then he was touching her.

As she cried out, his hips surged up and he cursed in a low, desperate sound, as if the feel of her was almost too much for him. It certainly was too much for her. She shattered apart, going rigid on top of his bare chest, her body torquing wildly as she climaxed. His mouth latched onto her throat and he sucked hard as he helped her ride out the sensations, his hand between her legs keeping her going.

When it was done, she collapsed against him, her face falling into his neck. She was limp as he rolled her over and she should have been embarrassed as she lay sprawled on the couch, but she just closed her eyes in bliss.

She felt the sofa wiggle as he stood up. Heard the shift of cloth as he took off his boxers. Then there was a soft tearing sound.

He stretched out on top of her, splitting her thighs

with his knees. His skin was griddle hot, his body flexed and straining with his need to finish.

At the first blunt brush of his arousal, her eyes popped wide.

"You're protected," he said. "I took care of it."

Her lids settled and she ran her hands up his thick shoulders. As his hips began rocking against her, he stared over her head, his face dark with concentration and barely leashed energy.

He went slowly, but even still she had to wince. In spite of how careful he was, and even though her body wanted him, the discomfort made her stiffen beneath him.

He stopped. Retreated a little. "Lizzie?"

Before he could say anything else, she blurted, "It's been a while for me."

As he looked down at her, his eyes became remote. "How long?"

"A while." When he just stared at her, she whispered, "A year or two."

Now he was the one wincing.

With an abrupt shift, he lifted off her body, pulled a throw blanket over her and sat down at the far end of the couch. Putting his elbows on his knees, he rubbed his face then reached between his legs. There was a snapping sound as he pulled off the protection.

In the silence that followed, Lizzie tucked the blanket in tight to her neck and stared at him. She was pretty sure why he'd stopped. The question was whether he'd be honest.

"I'm sorry." He rubbed his face some more. "I don't want to use you for sex, just to get rid of that dream."

As if that was the only reason he'd wanted to be with her. *Ouch*.

And damn, she hated being right. Good thing they'd stopped when they had.

She sat up, holding the blanket to her breasts and thinking she had to get out of this apartment fast. Thank heavens her T-shirt was right on the floor next to the couch. She picked it up and managed to get it on even though her hands were shaking. Where were her panties—oh. They were unwearable.

She got to her feet and wrapped the blanket around her hips, prepared to leave without another word.

Except then he said, "Can I come with you?"

She looked over at him. "What do you mean?"

"Can I, ah… Can I sleep with you? As in sleep, sleep with you?" He glanced up at her. "God, that sounds lame."

Her first and only thought was…she would love to have him in her bed like that.

He cursed and muttered, "Forget—"

"Yes." She held out her hand. "Yes, you can."

As Sean settled into Lizzie's bed, he let out a deep sigh. Man, this was good. The sheets smelled like her and so did the pillow his head was on. From over on the left, the rain softly hitting the window made him think of cats padding over hardwood floors. Lightning still flashed and thunder still rolled, but the storm was winding down.

This was better than good.

Lizzie came in with two glasses of water. She put

one on the bedside table next to him and took the other around to her side. She was awkward and lovely as she dropped the throw blanket and scooted under the covers with him. Then the lights went off and they were together in the dark.

He turned toward her, feeling needy and hating himself. "Can I hold you?"

She rolled right into him and he fit her warmth to his body, tucking her head under his chin, intertwining his legs with hers.

"What sort of nightmare was it?" she asked.

"The old kind." Yeah, the really old kind. The one where his father came into his room after he'd finished off with Mac. Mac had always been able to take a lot, but sometimes he broke and then it was Sean's turn, if their father was still angry. As the third in line, Billy had almost never been worked over. He'd just had to listen to the sounds and wonder if he was going to be next.

Which had been a head screw nonetheless.

Man, the not knowing had been the worst. You never knew whether it was going to be this night or another…. Whether the monster was going to come after you because your brother couldn't handle it… If it was going to hurt less or more than before—

"Are you cold?" Lizzie asked, inching even closer to him. "You're shivering."

Sean squeezed his eyes shut and wondered what all those people on Wall Street would think if they could see him now, curled up for comfort against a woman he barely knew because she was all he had to turn to.

He kissed Lizzie's hair then rubbed his face against it, dragging himself back from where he'd been.

Unfortunately, what he tuned into was her body.

Upstairs, his response to her had been all about pent-up fear and anger, an unleashing. But now in this quiet room, with the storm outside receding and the soft dripping of rain all that was left of the weather's fury, he found himself wanting to make love to her, not just have sex with her.

His body began to hurt with need denied and now renewed.

Except he knew it was wrong. Over the next couple of weeks, he was going to pack up the apartment upstairs, sell the house and never look back. Meanwhile, she was a woman who wasn't into short-term lovers—her history said it all.

"Sean?" she whispered into his neck.

The brush of her breath against his skin made him jerk. And his reply was nothing more than a growl.

Her palm slid over his waist and down to his hips and… He hissed sharply as she found the ache behind the boxers he'd thrown on.

Unconsciously, his hips moved, pressing his flesh into her grip. But then he reached down and brought her hand to his lips. Looking into her eyes, falling into them, he wanted her in ways he couldn't name. Refused to name.

God…maybe he was protecting himself, as well, by not being with her.

"Lizzie—"

"At least let me…take care of you. Your body isn't going to let you sleep."

He went still, lungs ceasing to draw. Oh, man, he wanted her to make him finish and not just because she was right about the not sleeping. He wanted her to be in charge of him.

Slowly, he put her hand back where it had been.

Lizzie urged him over onto his back, and as he complied, she pulled the sheets free of his body. Going up on her knees, blond hair falling forward, shirt hanging loose, she reached down and dragged his boxers off his legs. His arousal landed flat on his belly, swollen and straining.

She came up to his mouth and kissed him with the sweet, hesitant style of a woman more passionate than experienced.

And it was just about the most erotic thing he'd ever had done to him. Many women had touched his body over the years; ever since he was sixteen and had embarked on his sexual life, he'd had no shortage of lovers. And yet he couldn't remember feeling so delighted by one. Or so turned-on.

"How do you like to be…" She couldn't finish the sentence.

He put his hands up to her face, feeling the burn in her cheeks. "Do what you like to me. I'll love it, whatever it is."

Sean gasped as she took him in hand then moved down his body. With a rush of breath, he let his head fall back onto the pillow and balled the sheets in his fists. He gave himself to her with no barriers, nothing contrived, no calculated sensual tricks.

In return, she gave him…everything.

At the last moment, just before he went over the edge, he pulled her up to his mouth. As he spilled himself into her hands, he kissed the lips that had pleasured him.

For some completely ridiculous reason, he found himself wanting to weep.

When morning came, Lizzie woke up in a furnace.

Okay, not a furnace. She was under a thin sheet and on her bed…. She just *felt* as if she were in an industrial boiler.

But she was very okay with the heat.

Sean had chased her over to the far edge of the mattress, snuggling up so close he might as well have been under her own skin. His chest was against her back, his head tucked into her nape, his legs twisted around hers.

She chuckled, thinking she now knew what pretzels felt like.

"I'm crowding you, aren't I?" he said in a lazy, gravelly voice.

"I don't mind at all."

"Good." His hand smoothed down her arm, found her palm and gave it a squeeze. Then he somehow managed to get even closer.

Which gave her a clear impression that however sleepy he was, there was one part of him that was wide-awake. With a soft growl, he rubbed that part in a slow circle against her bottom. When she gasped and arched into him, he made a purring sound.

"You're hell on my good intentions there, Lizzie."

His voice vibrated in his chest as he nuzzled the back of her neck. "Pure hell."

"Am I?" She deliberately moved with him and smiled at the rumbling curse she got in response.

"You know you are." His lips traveled to her shoulder and he sank his teeth into her, tugging a little then sucking the spot through her T-shirt. "You treated me fine in this bed last night."

God, she loved that South Boston accent of his, that rough tone, that need. "Just returning the favor," she murmured.

"So I guess it's my turn again, Lizzie." His hand slipped under her shirt and found her breast. "I'm wicked tired, though. Guess I'll have to go real slow."

He shifted down her body, tunneling under the sheets, rolling her onto her stomach. His mouth found her spine and followed it all the way to her—

The phone rang with an ear-splitting peal.

Sean paused, but didn't stop.

Unfortunately, neither did the phone. And what if it was her mother having burned the house down or given the car away or done any one of a thousand things that spelled disaster?

As Lizzie stretched up to the bedside table and popped the phone off the cradle, Sean's response was to start in on the backs of her thighs.

Man, if this was a telemarketer, she was going rip his or her head off. "Hello?"

"Lizzie, it's perfect!"

"Mom?" Thankfully, Sean eased up and she caught her breath. "Mom...now's not a good t—"

"The kiln is working beautifully!"

"It's working...*what?*" Lizzie looked at the alarm clock with panic. Eleven. Eleven o'clock...oh God, she and Sean had overslept and the kiln had been delivered and her mother was now using the thing so the chances of getting the art store to take it back were next to nil. "Mom—"

"I'm positively inspired.... The wings of creation are fanning me...." As her mother started in on one of her soliloquies about artistic vision, Lizzie just let her go on.

All she could think about right now was that two thousand dollars they'd lost.

The call didn't so much end as flame out, with her mother getting more and more caught up in her own excitement until she had to go express herself.

As Lizzie hung up, Sean appeared from under the sheets, his dark hair tousled. "Trouble with mom?"

"Nothing unusual. Unfortunately."

He eased onto his side and propped his head up with his hand, the gold cross around his neck lying flat on the mattress.

He ran his finger down her cheek. "You know something, Lizzie, I have an idea."

"What?"

"Let's play hooky today."

"Hooky?"

"Yeah, let's grab some eats and a blanket and drive over to Esplanade. We can sit by the river and just forget about everything." When she hesitated, he murmured, "Unless you have other plans?"

While she thought about the day, he idly lifted her hand to his mouth and sucked her forefinger between his lips. As he swirled his tongue around, the circling movement was liquid and warm and oh so smooth. His eyes flipped to her face and he stared at her from under heavy lids.

Other plans? As if her job search couldn't wait until tomorrow?

"No…" she said. "I don't have anything I have to do."

He released her finger and slowly rolled on top of her, his body flowing over hers, a heavy weight full of strength. As his thigh fell between her knees, she yielded to him.

He suspended his torso on muscular arms and looked down into her face, hovering above her like some great bird of prey, all latent power. With the way he looked at her now, he made her feel marked and she knew then without a doubt they were going to be together.

Even though he would leave and never look back and she would miss him for a long, long time, she was going to have him.

He dropped down and kissed her lightly. "I'll see you in twenty minutes."

When she nodded, he leaped out of bed and disappeared through the door.

Before she got up, she made two quick phone calls. One was to the art store's manager, who confirmed there was no returning the kiln now that her mother had used it. The other was to the bank, which informed her that her only option to keep the check from bouncing was to do a credit-card transfer.

Two thousand dollars at nineteen-percent interest. Terrific.

She hung up the phone and told herself that at least the kiln could be sold when her mother moved on to her next big inspiration.

So everything was going to be okay. Eventually.

Chapter Seven

Lounging beneath a blue sky dotted with cotton-ball clouds, Sean stretched his legs straight out in front of him and crossed his ankles. Lizzie was next to him on the plaid blanket, curled on her side, eyes closed, a little smile on her mouth.

Life was just about perfect right now, he thought.

After they'd staked out a stretch of grass on the Esplanade, they'd had turkey subs for lunch and backed up the foot-longs with oatmeal cookies the size of hubcaps. Now, in spite of the shouts from some guys playing Frisbee and the barking of dogs and the occasional horn on Storrow Drive, Lizzie was fading like a sunset.

And just as lovely.

Abruptly, he thought about all the hours she pulled

between being at the clinic and moonlighting downtown. He frowned. Although he respected people who worked as hard and as long as he did, for some reason, Lizzie's going around the clock bothered him.

Probably because she seemed so delicate right now, the fine bones of her face showing too prominently under her pale skin.

She covered her mouth with the back of her hand and yawned. "I'd better sit up soon."

"The hell you should. Don't you know how to play hooky?"

She laughed and opened a pair of very sleepy green eyes. "I'm afraid I always followed the rules in school. So I'm not all that familiar with the hooky routine."

"Well, learn from the master. Hooky means you do whatever you want. And I'm no mind reader, but you look like you're really jonesing for a nap."

"I am." She yawned again and smiled up at him. "Were you a rebel in high school?"

"Yup." A rebel who had pulled As, but trouble nonetheless.

"And you still are, aren't you?"

He grinned at her. "My tattoo is an old one, I'll have you know."

"Except it's not the ink in your skin, it's your nature. I could tell by the way you looked at me that first night. You weren't all that interested in social pleasantries. But you weren't mean, though. Your father was the same way."

Sean's eyes shifted out to the Charles River. His father not mean? Yeah, right.

He felt his hand get gripped. "What happened with

your dad, Sean? I know you don't like to talk about it, but…"

As her words drifted, he absently rubbed her palm with his thumb and watched a crew boat stroke under one of the bridges that stretched over the water. Eventually, he said, "Nothing happened that matters now. It's all over and done."

"Do your brothers feel the same way?"

"Yeah." Although actually, he didn't know that for sure. None of them had ever talked about it. Especially Mac, who'd taken the lion's share of the abuse.

"Do you see your brothers often?"

Sean smiled a little. "Billy and I are tight. He comes down to the city a lot on the off season and we have a great time."

"Off season?"

"He's a football player. Linebacker for the Patriots."

"Boy, what a life that must be."

"Yeah, he gets around. And I'm not just talking about all the traveling he does. My brother's a real ladies' man, but he's also a spectacular athlete. Think the world of the guy, I really do."

"And your other brother?"

Sean shrugged. "I love him just as much, but no one knows Mac well, not even us."

"What does he do?"

"He's in the army. Special forces." At least that was the story. Mac had been very quiet about his job so both his brothers suspected he was involved in some very high-level covert ops.

Yeah…there was some possibility Mac was an

assassin. Although that was based on one dropped comment made years ago.

"Where does Mac live?"

"He has a place just outside of D.C., but he's not there all that often." Not there at all, frankly.

"What was your mother like?"

"She died when I was very young."

Lizzie lifted her head. "I'm so sorry. Do you remember anything about her?"

Sean broke the contact of their hands. The idea that secrets were escaping him, that revelations were being made that he couldn't retract, that she was getting into his head, made him twitchy. In the home he'd grown up in, and in the profession he excelled at, vulnerabilities were used against you.

Silence was safety.

He brushed his finger down her straight, slightly freckled nose. "So how about that nap for you?"

She smiled and closed her eyes. "I'll stop prying."

In the silence that followed, Sean frowned, thinking there had been no censure in her tone. Just acceptance. The fact that she didn't get on him made him feel grateful…and even closer to her.

"You don't mind?" he said softly. "That I'm not a big talker?"

"Not at all, Sean. Just being out in the sun with you is enough for me."

He stared down at her for the longest time, thinking how perverse it was that now that he knew she didn't care whether he said another thing, he found himself wanting to talk.

He looked back out to the river and watched the sun glimmer across the Charles with poetic glory, all golden sparkles over gentle waves. On the far side of the water was Harvard, that mountain of red brick and wrought-iron fencing. His eyes shifted up to the bright-blue dome that marked the horizon.

"I liked school and I was good at it," he said for no particular reason. "I liked reading and studying. Liked to see my report cards. Liked to be at the top of my class. In high school, I would have graduated valedictorian, but I got arrested for stealing a car my junior year and that took me out of the running no matter how high my GPA was. Yeah…school was all I had really, growing up. The only constant."

When there was no response, he glanced down. Lizzie was sleeping soundly, her eyelids flickering a little as if she were dreaming.

He told himself it was just as well. Didn't quite believe it.

Taking a page from Lizzie's book, he lay all the way down and rested his head on the back of his forearm. As a sailboat bobbed by right in front of them, he had some dim thought that he hadn't had a vacation in…ever? How was that possible?

Surely he'd taken a week. A long weekend. Something.

Good God, no, he hadn't. He'd worked through his college vacations as a member of the grounds crew to make extra money. Then in the years that had followed, he'd been too busy getting an MBA and making a name for himself. Now, any traveling he did was for business:

captive insurance meetings in the Bahamas or the Caymans, trips to Tokyo and London and Hamburg and South America, financial summits in Switzerland. And as for the triathalons he entered? That was still all about competing and winning, not recreation.

Hell, he couldn't remember the last time he'd done something like this…. Just sat on the grass and let his thoughts drift with the breeze.

"Heads up!" someone hollered.

Sean glanced to the right and saw a Frisbee flying through the air, heading straight for Lizzie.

Lizzie heard a curse and then felt herself get covered by the weight of Sean's body. As her eyes flipped open, she saw him deftly catch a Frisbee…that would have hit her right in the face.

"Sorry, man!" a guy said as he ran over. "Everyone okay?"

Sean balanced his upper body on one arm as he reached up to give the thing back. "Yeah. Watch it though."

"We will," the guy promised. "Hey, great save, by the way. Wanna play?"

The light that came into Sean's eyes made Lizzie smile. "Go ahead," she said. "I'm sure you're terrific at it."

The guy with the Frisbee looked at her. "And you're welcome, too."

"Thanks, but I'd rather be on blanket patrol."

"You don't mind?" Sean asked her with a frown.

"Not at all."

"Okay. I won't be long, though." He kissed her quick

and leaped to his feet. In a smooth move, he took off his shirt and let it fall to the blanket. "Don't want to get this sweated out in case we head off to dinner."

Sean jogged over with the guy and shook hands with the other players. On the bright green grass, he fit in perfectly with them, one more strong set of shoulders, one more defined chest. The bunch of them went at it hard, until there were three disks going at once between five guys. Sean was amazing, all lithe power and razor instincts, his big body moving with elegant speed, his loose jeans hanging low on his hips, his gold cross bouncing against his chest as he ran around.

Those red and yellow Frisbees went faster and faster and the guys got more outrageous. Eventually, Sean went for a flying catch, springing up into the air and going horizontal to the ground—right as another guy came from the opposite direction. The two collided and fell hard.

Lizzie started to scramble to her feet…but they were fine as they rolled onto their backs and laughed. As she took a deep breath, Sean flashed her a thumbs-up then stood and went back into the fray.

While the horsing around went on, she felt as if she were playing with him even though she was on the blanket. Every few minutes or so, he would look over at her and wave. Or wink. Or he'd deliberately run by and do some wild catch around his back or pull off a crazy, convoluted toss.

He was showing off. For her.

Which was pretty darned charming.

By the time he came back to the blanket forty-five

minutes later, he was breathing hard and a sheen of sweat covered his smooth skin.

"That was great," he said. "Thanks." He sat down, putting his forearms on his knees to air himself out as he regained his breath.

God, she wanted him. "You looked like you were having a wonderful time."

"It's been a while since I've just run around for no good reason." He reached into the Deluca's paper bag and took out a Poland Spring bottle. As he cracked the top, he shot her a quick smile then tilted his head back and poured the water down his throat, his Adam's apple working in a rhythm.

When he brought his head back to level, he pointed at her, bottle in hand. "So what can we do for you? I mean, I've had my fun. We should do something you want to now."

As she considered the offer, she prayed he couldn't read minds. Because all she could think of was him moving down her body this morning…and how much she wanted him to do that again. Without interruption.

Sean frowned. "Hey, do you have enough sunscreen on? You look a little red."

Uh-huh. Go figure. "Ice cream."

"I'm sorry?"

"I would love some ice cream." She put her hand on her stomach. "Even though I shouldn't—"

"Ice cream it is." He finished the water and sprang to his feet as if he hadn't just run miles chasing a Frisbee. "You have a favorite place?"

"I'm easy." Lizzie got up as he tucked his shirt into

the back pocket of his jeans and together they folded the blanket. "As long as it's cold and sweet, I'm happy."

Just as they were about to leave, she frowned. "Wait a minute."

"What?"

She looked around. She had her purse and he had the blanket and the bag of food and they'd left no trash. But something was off.

When she ran her eyes up and down his chest, she realized what it was. "Your cross. It's missing."

Sean's hand snapped to his heart, and though he tried to fight it, she could see panic in his eyes.

"Don't worry, we'll find it," she told him.

They walked the area he'd played in, but it seemed hopeless as he'd covered a lot of distance during the game. Then she remembered. Where had he fallen with the other guy? She headed over to where she thought he'd hit the ground and began crisscrossing the vicinity.

She was about to give up when she saw a flash of gold in the cropped blades of grass. "I've got it!"

Sean came running over and as she held out her hand he sagged in relief. He took the necklace and inspected the clasp, then put it back on.

"Don't know how it fell off," he said. "Everything seems okay."

"You should get it checked."

"I will." His hazel eyes lifted and met hers, then he bent down and kissed her. "Thank you," he whispered against her mouth. "Just…yeah, thank you."

"You're welcome." As he pulled back, he was

gripping the cross so hard his knuckles were white. "It obviously means a great deal to you."

He glanced down. "Mac gave one to me and to Billy and kept a third for himself. I wear it because…hell, I don't know."

Abruptly, his lids dropped over eyes that had gone deliberately blank.

She squeezed his hand. "Let's go."

Sean kept it together as they walked away from where the necklace had been lost, but he cracked a couple minutes later.

The two of them were on the Arthur Fiedler pedestrian bridge that arched over Storrow Drive when he put his arm around Lizzie's shoulders and drew her tight to his side. A few feet farther and he stopped altogether, gathered her in his arms and put his mouth to her ear.

"Lizzie?"

"Yes?"

"If I had lost that necklace…it would have killed me."

"I'm so glad we found it." As she hugged him, he absorbed her kindness, fed off it.

"Mac got the crosses for us right after he went through basic training and before he shipped out for the first time." Sean kept speaking right into her ear, the only way he could continue. "I haven't seen him in a decade and I talk to him once a year if I'm lucky…when he calls me on my birthday. So the necklace is all I have of him. Lose it, lose him." Sean cursed as he heard what he was saying and pulled back. "Sorry, don't mean to get melodramatic."

Her arms tightened around his waist. "You're not."

Looking into her eyes, he felt as though the essential loneliness of his life was exposed, laid bare to the summer day and to her. For all the people he dealt with every hour of the week, for all the women he'd been with and the men he competed against, he was nonetheless alone.

Except he didn't feel alone now.

He kissed Lizzie at first just in thanks for her understanding and acceptance. Then he kissed her some more because he didn't want to stop.

As the sun fell on his bare shoulders and people walked by and cars zoomed underneath them, he dropped the bag and the blanket he was carrying, dug his hands into her hair and tilted her head back so he could go deeper into her. In response, she settled against him like warm water, flowing over his hard edges, both soothing him and exciting him.

He closed his eyes and let himself get good and lost in her. Oh, man, did he have plans for them. Tonight, he was going to go back to her apartment and make love to her. Slowly. Thoroughly. He was after the closeness, not just the orgasms, and he was going to hold her afterward until he was ready to do it again. Then he was going to sleep next to her and wake up looking into her face.

When he finally pulled back from her mouth, he brushed her lower lip with his thumb. "I can't feel my legs. How about you?"

She laughed a little breathlessly. "I'm on fire."

"Then we'd better cool you down." He kissed her quick. "How's Ben & Jerry's sound?"

"Perfect. I'd love some of their Mint Oreo in a waffle cone."

"Ask and ye shall receive."

They meandered off the bridge and hooked up with Newbury Street, joining the crowd that strolled down the sidewalk. There was a line in front of Ben & Jerry's, but the breeze was nice and soon enough their cones were being handed to them. As he pulled a twenty out of his wallet, Lizzie went for her purse.

"No, wait. Let me—"

"My treat," he said. After he gave the bill to the kid behind the register, he nodded to the door. "Shall we?"

The kid called out, "Don't you want your change?"

"Yeah. In the tips jar."

"Hey, thanks, man!"

Sean smiled and followed Lizzie out into the sun.

"I really like that about you," she said as she stuck a white spoon into her waffle cone and brought some of the chunky ice cream to her mouth.

"Like what?"

"That you tip generously. Mmm, this is so good."

Sean watched her lick her spoon clean and had to put the blanket in front of his hips. God, men were letches, weren't they? But man…he wanted her.

He cleared his throat. What had they been talking about? Oh, yeah… "Well, I know what it's like to live off tips. I've waited a lot of tables in my day—"

"Sean? Sean O'Banyon?"

Sean frowned at the male voice and looked over his shoulder. When he saw who it was, he felt an absurd impulse to shield Lizzie, to protect their day together.

Except it was too late. As a well-dressed man headed right for them, he knew that the bubble he'd been in all afternoon was about to burst.

Chapter Eight

Lizzie smiled at the gentleman who was hustling up to them. He looked very *Great Gatsby* in his white linen slacks, crisp blue button-down and navy-blue blazer with a kerchief in the pocket. His loafers were shiny and tasseled and his round glasses were made of tortoiseshell.

He looked very pleased to see Sean. "Sean! How do? I haven't seen you since—"

"Rolly, it's good to see you." Sean stuck his hand out. "How are you?"

"Fine, fine. And you? I've heard you're doing great things with—"

"So how is it possible you're in town on a sunny Saturday? Is the whole family here with you, too?"

"No, no. Sarah and the kids are at the house on the

Vineyard, lucky devils. I had to come in for business. I'm sure you know how that—"

"I'd like you to meet my friend, Lizzie. Lizzie, this is Rolly."

The man smiled, revealing perfect teeth. "Good Lord, where are my manners? It's a pleasure."

Lizzie shoved her spoon into her cone and offered her hand. "Nice to meet you."

"Enjoying the day with Sean, are you?" he said as they shook.

"Very much."

"You know, I didn't think the great SOB ever wandered around—"

"You need to give my regards to Sarah," Sean cut in.

"Of course, and I hope you'll come out and visit us sometime on the Vineyard?" Rolly smiled at Lizzie. "Friends are always welcome, too. We have a big house and the more the merrier. Well, I must off to the club. I'm late, which I despise."

As the man waved and dissolved into the pedestrian stream, Lizzie glanced at Sean. His brows were down low and his mouth set tight.

She was not surprised when he said, "How about we head home? I could use a shower."

"Sounds good," she said. Even though it didn't. She wasn't in a hurry for the day to end, but she sensed that even if they kept walking around now, it would be over anyway. Sean had gone somewhere in his head and his mood had changed. Which was odd. Rolly Whoever-he-was had seemed perfectly nice, yet Sean had been in a hurry to get rid of him.

They were quiet as they walked down Newbury then went through the Commons and down into the parking garage. Sean didn't say much on the way home, and when they pulled up to the row house, she had a feeling he was going to make an excuse to go upstairs.

She told herself it was better this way as she could start getting her résumés out.

Yeah…right.

As they got out of the car and went up to the shallow front porch, she said, "Well, thank you for the day. I had a wonderful time."

Sean stopped. Looked her in the eye. Took her hand in his. "I'm sorry, Lizzie. About being a buzz kill."

"Why did running into that man bother you so much?"

Sean glanced across the street, but she was sure he wasn't seeing the other row houses. "He and I went to college together." In a dry voice, he added, "I was on scholarship, Rolly wasn't."

Oh, that explained it. It must be hard to see people who were so much more successful, who had so much more.

"Money isn't everything, Sean."

He smiled his disagreement. "Sometimes it feels that way. Sometimes I think my whole life is about chasing the stuff."

"I totally get that," she said as she thought about her mom. "But come on, how much did today cost us? The two sandwiches were eight bucks. The cookies were what…four dollars? A six-pack of water was a dollar ninety…on sale, I might remind you. And the cones were nine dollars with an eleven-dollar tip. For thirty-three dollars and ninety cents, which could have been even less if you hadn't left so much at Ben & Jerry's, we had a perfectly lovely afternoon. After all, the sun and the Frisbee game were—"

He swooped in and kissed her, his mouth lingering on hers before he pulled back.

"—free," she finished.

Sean ran his fingertip down her cheek then took a deep breath, as if he were bracing himself for something. "So you wouldn't think of me differently, rich or poor?"

"I enjoyed today because of you. The fact that you're not wealthy never even occurred to me."

His eyes grew shrewd as if he were assessing her down to her DNA. Then he nodded once, took out his keys and put one in the lock. When he paused, his stare shifted over to hers and the hazel in it burned.

"Do you want to get together tonight?" he asked in a very low voice.

Lizzie swallowed hard, knowing very well what it meant to say yes to the question. She took a deep breath. "Yes."

"I'll come down right after I shower."

He pushed the door wide and held it open for her. As she walked by him, a horrible realization hit her and she wanted to curse.

Oh God…in the space of two days, she'd somehow become attached to this man.

And she feared there was no going back.

* * *

In the shower upstairs, Sean soaped his body up and rinsed off as if he were an Indy 500 pit crew. He shaved just as fast and managed to nick himself under the chin, which necessitated tearing off a piece of Kleenex and sticking it to where he bled. After brushing his wet hair back, he did the cologne thing and inspected the razor cut.

With relief, he ditched the little white square. Man, there was no looking good with that kind of thing on your puss.

Boxers went on without incident as did a fresh black polo. Pants were an issue because his jeans were grass-stained, so in the end, he pulled on his suit slacks. Thank God they didn't have any pinstripes, so he didn't look ridiculous.

On his way out the door, he slipped a couple of condoms in his back pocket out of necessity and picked his BlackBerry up out of habit.

Oh…crap, he thought as he stared at the phone.

He couldn't believe he'd left the thing behind today. How had that happened?

Then again, the oversight had been a blessing. Part of the reason the afternoon had been so relaxing was that the ringer hadn't gone off constantly.

He flipped through the screens. He had an in-box full of e-mails and seven voice messages waiting for him. He almost started checking it all, but at the last moment, he stopped. He didn't want to know what was falling apart. All he wanted was just a little more time with Lizzie. Then he'd get back to real life.

Shoving it into his pocket, he left the apartment and

was at her door in three heartbeats. After he knocked once, he heard her call out and he went inside.

She ducked into the living room wrapped in nothing but a towel, her hair in damp ringlets. "Hi, I'll just get dress—"

She didn't have a chance to finish the sentence.

Sean went to her in two long strides, clamped his hands on either side of her face and dropped down, fusing his mouth to hers. As he pushed her back against the wall, he was hard, hot, hungry, his hands finding the edge of the towel and stripping it away.

With a quick move, he picked her up and carried her to her bed, laying her out flat on the comforter. He tore his shirt over his head, kicked off his shoes and covered her body with his own, all but out of control as he kissed her deep and long. He kept at it until they were both breathless, then went to work on her neck.

"I need to…" His voice cracked as he palmed her hip and squeezed. "I need to be inside you."

She nodded with a jerky head bob then dug her hands into his hair and pulled him up to her mouth again. It was the perfect move because he couldn't get enough of her lips, her scent, her crazy moaning…. The way her legs were scissoring underneath his was driving him insane.

Somehow, his pants disappeared along with his boxers. He wasn't sure how and didn't care; maybe the damn things walked off his legs by their own volition. What mattered was that he and Lizzie were both wild and naked and he was pressing into the soft space between her thighs with razor-edged desperation.

He needed this so badly. He needed *her* so badly.

* * *

Sean was all carnal demand and Lizzie loved it. Especially when his fully naked body came down on hers and his thighs split her open to him. His skin burned as if he had a fever and his hands were rough and his mouth was hungry and he was going to take her hard just the way she wanted him to. It was the kind of full-tilt sex she'd only heard about and had assumed was wildly exaggerated.

And yet as she cried out, he went still. "Lizzie…I'm sorry. I'm so sorry. I'm going too f—"

She locked her legs around his hips and went for his mouth, frantic for more of him. As her tongue pierced his lips, he groaned wildly and his arms shot around her, his hips falling into a grinding rhythm that blinded her. Everything was fast, fast and edgy and just a little reckless, nothing she was used to and everything she wanted.

"Lizzie…can I—"

"Yes."

He reared back and rose off her, his arousal jutting out from his hips, proud and ready. He ripped a condom wrapper open with his sharp white teeth, spit out the corner, then he sheathed himself with quick, sure hands. His heavy weight came back down on her and she trembled, ready, but bracing herself for a powerful thrust.

Instead, he eased into her. As they slowly came together, his head dropped down beside hers so they were ear to ear.

"Are you okay?" he asked hoarsely. "This okay?"

His ragged breath and the sweat on his skin gave her an idea how much his self-control was costing him.

She dug her nails into the small of his back and arched. "More."

With one smooth push, he locked his hips against hers and they both moaned as their pelvises merged. Their bodies took over, meeting and retreating, his advancing, hers receiving. As he moved inside of her, his muscles bunched and relaxed in his shoulders and his legs, and his slick skin slid over hers. The rhythm of it all intensified until she was nothing but sensation and instinct.

"Lizzie…Lizzie, I'm about to—"

A phone started ringing right by the bed, but it wasn't one of hers.

As it went off again, Sean froze then cursed and squeezed his eyes shut.

She cleared her throat. "Ah…do you want to get that?"

His answer was a straight, to the point expletive followed by the word *no*.

As the ringer kept going off, he resumed pumping, falling into a driving, primal pace that took her right over the edge. As she soared beneath him, he fell over the brink himself, his head tilting back, his neck straining. He roared, more beast than man in the beautiful moment that he gave himself to her.

When he stopped bucking against her, he collapsed, his heart pounding so hard she could feel every beat in her own chest.

With the phone now silent, the only sound in the room was their breathing.

As passion's heat faded from their bodies, her chest ached although she wasn't sure why.

* * *

Sean was utterly sated as he rolled to the side and took Lizzie with him. Looking into her face, her eyes were so clear and guileless he wondered how he could have ever thought she was calculating, and he loved that she was so transparent.

What he didn't like was the fact that she seemed a little rattled.

"Lizzie…" He kissed her softly. "You okay there?"

She ran her hand up the back of his arm and nodded.

"Lizzie? Did I hurt you?"

"Oh…no…it's not that."

"Talk to me."

"I…ah, I didn't know…" Her eyes dropped. "I didn't know it could be like that."

Sean went utterly still; he didn't even breathe. Time became a meaningless measure of nothing important. "Lizzie—"

His cell phone went off again, the soft tone landing like a bomb.

With a curse, he shot out of bed and grabbed his boxers, holding them in front of his hips as he headed for his pants.

"What?" he snapped as he answered the damn thing.

"Where the *hell* have you been?" Ah yes, Mick Rhodes. Lawyer. Friend. And when in that tone of voice, bearer of bad news.

"Just spit it," Sean muttered. "What's on fire?"

"Condi-Foods. Name ring a bell? Damn it, I called you five times this afternoon. Where have you been? You know the deal is shaky—"

"Skip the lecture and give me details."

Mick swore a couple of times then launched into a news flash that set Sean's teeth on edge. "The revised tender offer from the acquirer is coming in two hours from now. Condi-Foods' board chair wants you and only you to render the opinion and he wants to hear it in person. So you need to drop whatever you're doing and get your ass into Manhattan *now*."

Sean cursed and reached back down for his trousers. Then realized he wasn't getting dressed unless he made a quick trip to the bathroom. "I'm on my way."

"Hey, there's an idea—"

"I'll call you from the plane." Sean hung up. Dropped his arm. Looked over his shoulder. "I have to go."

"Was that your boss?"

"Basically." Actually, he was Mick's boss, as he'd hired the guy to work on the legal aspects of these deals. But his pal was right to goose him. He'd left a two-billion-dollar negotiation hanging in the breeze today. So he could play Frisbee for God's sake.

Not a smart career move. Or a responsible one.

Sean went into the bathroom, snapped off the condom and washed up. Without looking at himself in the mirror, he put on his boxers and his pants and headed back to the bedroom.

"I'm really sorry about this," he said, picking up his shirt from the floor. He pulled it over his head and shoved his feet into his running shoes. "I'll call you."

Lizzie's eyes grew remote. "Have a safe trip."

"Lizzie, I'll call you. I promise."

She smiled slowly. "Okay…I'd like that. I'd really like that."

Chapter Nine

Four nights later, in a conference room high above Wall Street, Sean lost it. Just *lost* it. And not in a calculated way intended to impact difficult negotiations.

He simply hit the wall. Then plowed right through it.

"To hell with this." He planted his big hands on the glossy mahogany table and rose from his seat. Leaning into his arms, he glared good and hard at the idiots who were wasting his and Condi-Foods' time. "Get out."

The head of the acquirer's investment team blinked like a bad lightbulb in his Brooks Brothers suit. "Excuse me?"

"Get. Out." This meeting had been a bad idea to begin with, but as the deal was at a standstill, Sean had agreed to the request for some face-to-face. He was not surprised they remained deadlocked, but it sure as hell didn't put him in a good mood.

Then again, since he'd left Lizzie's Saturday night, nothing had given him a jolly.

"Our share price is fair!" the man across the table hollered.

"No, it isn't, and it's backed up by air. You find yourself some better financing and come up on your number, then we'll talk."

"Damn it, O'Banyon! We've been working on this for the last four days—"

"And time has not improved your offer. Get. Out."

There was a long pause and then they just started yammering on again about their low-ball valuation of Condi-Foods' assets. One of them even had the nerve to push a spreadsheet at him.

Sean balled the thing up and tossed it into a waste-paper basket across the room.

Which effectively ended the meeting.

All six guys across the table stood up and, amid much huffing and offense, funneled out of the room as if the door were a drain. Before he left, the team leader glanced back at Sean. The man's eyes were shrewd and that was when Sean knew. What had just transpired was a test of his resolve by the opposing side, not any kind of genuine stalemate.

They were going to meet his demands. He could feel it. And as Mick Rhodes chuckled a little in the seat next to him, it was clear his buddy knew it, too.

In the aftermath of the drama bomb, Sean eased down into his chair.

As silence reigned, the two young guys he'd picked up from that gala, Freddie Wilcox and Andrew Frick, were frozen-statue speechless.

"Do we leave now?" Freddie asked.

"Nope," Mick replied. The lawyer's sardonic grin, which was as sharp as his Brioni suit, made a quick appearance. "Twenty-seven, SOB. Don't you think?"

Sean rubbed his face and played along out of habit, not because he was interested in the game. "Thirty-nine. Because I balled their—what did I throw?"

Andrew spoke up. "I believe it was their financial projections for the coming fiscal year."

"Ah, then I put them in the right place." Sean leaned back in his chair and rolled his Montblanc between his thumb and forefinger. The fountain pen was one of his signature props, a big black cigar of a writing instrument known on Wall Street as the Club for all the damage he'd done with it.

Usually at this point, when he knew in his gut he was going to get what he wanted, he'd feel a simmering triumph. After all, making the other side break and submit was the goal, and sure as hell, those highfliers who'd just fluffed out of here were going to call back within the hour with a reasonable offer that he could recommend to the Condi-Foods board.

He'd been through this countless times. It was the cycle of challenge that had kept him juiced for years.

But the problem was, on this particular walk through the minefield, he really had lost his temper. Unlike the other side, his anger hadn't been for show. His frustration level had been on hard-boil since he'd come back to the city and now he was stretched as thin as a hair. The three-ring circus of these negotiations, coupled with that grossly inadequate offer, had just pushed him over the edge.

And there was nothing more dangerous in a multi-billion-dollar negotiation than one of the principals getting truly emotional.

He told himself he was just strung out. Hell, he'd been working until three in the morning every night since he'd come back, and although that wasn't unprecedented, it certainly didn't put him in his happy place. Plus the fact that these negotiations had been going so slowly made it all worse—

Oh, who was he kidding. It wasn't business that was razoring him up.

His conscience was wearing on him. Badly.

Lizzie Bond was wearing on him.

He got to his feet and started to pack up his briefcase.

"You're leaving?" Mick said.

"I already know what they're going to do." Sean slipped the Club into his breast pocket then text messaged his limo driver. "They're going to come up twenty-five cents a share and get real on the interest payments before the balloon five years out of closing. And I will accept that. Call me when the new offer comes through."

Andrew cleared his throat. "But how do you know that's what they're going to counter with?"

Sean picked up his leather document holder. "Because it's the only move they have. If they back out after getting this close, everyone on the Street will think it's because they don't have the corporate will to be a player and that lack of confidence would be bad news for their stock. As usual it all comes down to pride and math."

The hero worship that flared in the kid's eyes was hard to bear so Sean looked around the room. "Ladies and gentlemen, it's been real. Mick, I'll be hearing from you shortly."

On his way out, he checked in with his assistants and picked up a stack of phone messages as well as the schedule for the next week and the so-called social file. When he told his staff he was going home, they looked relieved, as if they needed a break from him.

He didn't blame them in the slightest.

He hit the elevators and exited the building. His limousine was waiting out front in the sweltering heat and he slid into the air-conditioned backseat with relief. As the Lincoln eased into traffic, he opened the social file with no enthusiasm. The thing was stuffed with invitations to galas and messages from women and favors he was being asked. Typically he would run through the morass in about ten minutes, turf the RSVPs to his assistants and call back a couple of the ladies.

Instead, he closed the cover and took out his Black-Berry.

Lizzie's face came to him, as it had on a regular basis, and he rubbed the center of his chest.

He'd wanted to talk to her since landing in Manhattan, but he'd been dealing with one problem after another in the Condi-Foods negotiations. The way things had been going, the only time he had to himself was either well after midnight or just around noontime. Neither of which were good times to reach her.

He'd tried to leave messages, but had just ended up deleting them halfway through. Even though he'd spoken thousands of sentences since getting back to the city, he somehow couldn't find the words to let her know how much he was thinking about her. And the longer he went, the worse he choked.

He checked his watch. Nine o'clock at night.

Damn it, he had to call. Considering all the crap that was going down with Condi-Foods, he wasn't going to get back to Boston for another week. And that was assuming the acquirer's offer finally did make sense.

As his limo slowly progressed down Wall Street, he dialed his BlackBerry, put the thing up to his ear and loosened his tie.

After the second ring, Lizzie's voice came through loud and clear. "Hello?"

God, she was home. "Lizzie…"

"Oh…hi." There was a shuffling sound as if she were switching her receiver to her other hand. "How are you?"

He thought about all the ways to answer the question. The replies disturbed him because they were all about missing her. "Good. Busy."

"I'm sure you have been." Her voice was level. Calm.

"Work's been hectic." The limo came to a stop at a traffic light, a thoroughbred among the herd of taxi ponies. As it occurred to him that she'd be surprised he was sitting in something like the stretch Lincoln, he felt like a liar.

Maybe everything he was holding back from her, rather than his schedule, had been what had prevented him from calling.

Screw the *maybe*. "Lizzie, I need to tell you—"

"You don't have to explain. We had a lovely evening, not a relationship." Oh, man, her tone wasn't just level. It was impersonal.

"Are you near a computer?" he said.

"I—ah, yes."

"Do a search under the name Sean O'Banyon."

"Why?"

"I want you to know who I am."

"I already do."

"No, you don't." And he wasn't sure how to tell her without sounding like a pompous ass. "Sean O'Banyon. Do it."

He heard the sound of keys typing. Then silence.

He knew what the search engine would pull up: References to articles on him in the *Wall Street Journal*. *The New York Times*. *Forbes*. *Fortune*. *Time*. Interviews logged on MSNBC and CNN and the FOX News network. Books on finance that had his name in them.

"What is all this?" she murmured.

"Me."

More silence. "Guess you're really not a construction worker."

"No, I'm not."

"Clearly."

"Lizzie—"

"Hey, you met with the president, huh."

"I didn't tell you because—"

Her voice sharpened. "Because you didn't trust me. Or you thought I was beneath you. Which one was it?"

"I didn't know you."

"And I guess a week away has made me more knowable?"

"I just don't want to lie by omission anymore. It's not right."

He heard her exhale. Heard a mouse clicking. "God, you must have really hated your father."

"Excuse me?"

"Do you know how hard he struggled to pay for his medications and his doctor visits? I mean, I doubt it would even make a dent in—oh, look, here's your net worth. Yeah, whoa…wouldn't even be couch change to you."

"This has nothing to do with him."

"Yeah…and you know what? I don't think it has anything to do with me, either."

God, he wished he'd left a couple of messages on her phone. Maybe this would have been easier. "It does, though. Damn it, Lizzie—"

"Do you think I was after your father for money? You did, didn't you? And you figured if I knew you were loaded I'd glom on to you, too."

"Look, like I said, I didn't know you. And why wouldn't I be suspicious? You mean you've never heard of that kind of thing?"

"Hey, check this out. You gave away a million dollars last month to the Hall Foundation. How generous." Her voice grew heated. "Good Lord, Sean, do you have any idea how tough these last few years have been on your father? You could have helped him. You *should* have helped him."

Okay, that was not a good topic to get on, Sean thought. Because he couldn't be civil about the fact that his father had obviously *poor-little-old-me*'d her.

"I'm not going to discuss him."

"Oh, that's right. Closed-door policy on that."

"Lizzie, no offense, but you don't know a thing about my father."

"Funny, the same could be said of you. I don't think you knew him very well, either."

Sean's hand curled around his BlackBerry. As he fought to rein in his temper, he reminded himself that she had no way of knowing about the past and that people, even his father, could present many different faces to the world.

"Let's keep this just to us, Lizzie. We'll get further."

She exhaled sharply, which he didn't take as a good sign. "You know what? Let's forget about us going anywhere, okay? Let me know about the house sale when you can. Goodbye."

She hung up on him.

Sean let his head fall back against the plush leather seat. Closing his eyes, he tried to tell himself it was for the best. She stirred up too much in him. Went in too deep. Made him feel too much.

It was better to be alone than in chaos.

Taking a deep breath, he put his palm under his tie and rubbed his sternum.

Damn, his chest hurt.

When his BlackBerry went off, he answered it without looking at the caller ID.

Mick Rhodes was in midlaugh. "Twenty-two minutes. I win."

"What did they come back with?"

"Up twenty-five cents a share and much better financing, at least to my eye. You're a genius, SOB."

"Tell them to get the papers to me."

"Will do."

Genius? Sean thought as they hung up. What a crock of crap that was. He felt like anything but.

After she ended the call, Lizzie just stared at the photograph on her laptop's screen. It was a picture of Sean looking like a total power player: Black suit. White shirt. Red tie. A hard smile and harder eyes.

A stranger.

Oh, but then he'd been that before, hadn't he?

She glanced at the date. The photo had been taken at a gala on the night Mr. O'Banyon had died and she thought back to when she'd called Sean with the news. Evidently this fancy party had been the noise she'd heard in the background.

She shut off the computer to get away from the image and let herself sink back into the sofa.

All around her, everything seemed too quiet. The drone of the AC unit. The dulled murmur of a passing car. The soft wind catching a piece of siding and making it whistle.

She wished she had to go to work or had someplace

to go. The only thing she had here at home was a whole lot of smothering introspection that she could do without. Trouble was, she wasn't moonlighting until tomorrow night and she was not the bar-hopping type.

Exhausted and cranky, she headed for bed for lack of a better alternative, but she was pretty sure she wasn't going to sleep. Sure enough, as she turned off the light and lay back, the mattress beneath her felt as if it were stuffed with gravel and her sheets were like sandpaper against her skin.

Man…this thing with Sean was such a mess.

She'd spent the last four days waiting for the phone to ring, if she was home, or checking her message light first thing as she came in the door. Naturally, when she'd decided he was never going to call, he did…only to drop this news flash that he was a big shot.

A big shot who evidently hadn't had enough cash to spare for his father in spite of being on the Fortune 500 list. Which was just wrong. Granted, Mr. O'Banyon hadn't starved, but things could have been a lot easier on him if he'd had a visiting nurse and if his medical bills had been covered.

Lizzie pictured the photograph of Sean she'd just seen. How he must have laughed at her. Thinking that he was a construction worker—

The phone started to ring in the living room, the cheerful chirping sound coming down the hall as if the noise were skipping.

The first ring she ignored. The second ring she ignored. On the third, she almost got up, but then she let the call dump into voice mail.

She didn't care what he had to say.

Crossing her arms over her chest, she closed her eyes.

Three minutes of pulling the mummy routine and she was out in the living room, finding the phone. There was a message so she dialed into the system and held her breath.

Her mother's voice was excited: "I have had a break-through with the clay! My fingers are singing! This is such a revelation, which…"

Lizzie closed her eyes and let the message roll on. After she deleted it and hung up, she stared at the phone and knew going back to bed was not an option.

She went to the couch, fired up her laptop again and logged into the *Boston Globe*'s online classifieds site. Since she was not going to get some shut-eye anytime soon, she might as well focus on something that would help her.

Which stewing about Sean O'Banyon would defi-nitely not.

Plus it was about time she got into her job search. She'd moonlighted every day this week so she would earn some extra cash, but as a result, she hadn't been able to find time to apply for a new position.

Two hours later, she had her résumé updated and had made online submissions to four jobs: one down on the South Shore at Quincy Hospital's ED and one each to Boston Medical Center, New England Medical Center and Brigham & Women's.

Next she hit the apartment ads. Even if Sean wasn't going to sell the house right away, she had to get out of here. There were just too many memories. And now too many complications.

She braced herself for what she'd find. She knew that the Boston real-estate market for rentals was tight right now because of all the college students returning for school in August. And it would probably make more sense to wait until she knew where she would be working, but she figured it couldn't hurt to start looking this Sunday when there'd be some open houses scheduled.

Oh…*man*. Everything was so expensive compared to what she was paying now. Part of it was that Eddie had refused to raise her rent over the two years she'd been here. The other half was simply supply and demand coupled with inflation.

She put the laptop aside and stared out the bay window. With her job at the clinic ending tomorrow, she was relieved to have plenty of moonlighting work lined up. But that was not the way she wanted to live. Pulling night shifts on a regular basis really screwed up your life.

Besides, she had her sights set on bigger things than being a floor nurse. What she wanted to be, eventually, was her boss, Denisha Roberts. She wanted to run a clinic like the one in Roxbury, and to do that, she needed more education and some experience on the administration side of patient care.

Unfortunately, she had a feeling school was going to be delayed for a while.

She turned off the computer and the lights, then went over to the armchair in front of the big window. Sitting down, she curled her legs up under herself and let her head fall to the side. Through the slits in the blinds she saw the dark path of the road and the sidewalk's ghostly glow and the bulky outlines of the houses across the street. As the night went on, occasionally a car would float by like a boat on a still river, its headlights flaring white then its brake lights glowing red.

Funny how losing a job made you look over your life and reassess things.

And the ending of a relationship did that, too, didn't it?

Except, had she even had a relationship with Sean? Not really. Just a couple of days… Still, the effect was the same. In the quiet darkness, she found herself thinking back to her two earlier boyfriends. Neither one had come close to Sean for intensity. But then she couldn't imagine many men did.

Just her luck.

Lizzie was still sitting in the chair a couple of hours later when a car pulled up in front of the house. The headlights went off, one of its doors slammed and a huge shadow of a man came up the walkway.

She got to her feet in disbelief and went to the blinds. Sean couldn't possibly have come all the way up from New York. In the middle of the night. Could he?

Good…Lord, he had.

In the glow of the porch light, he looked totally out of place, more like he should be walking up to the door of a Park Avenue penthouse rather than a well-worn duplex in South Boston. He was wearing a beautifully tailored dark suit with a fancy black-and-peach–colored tie, and as he reached forward to put his key in the lock, a big fat gold watch gleamed on his wrist.

Lizzie stepped back from the window. Maybe he hadn't come to see—

The knock on her door was a single, sharp rap.

His voice came through the panels. "Lizzie, I saw you at the blinds. I know you're up. Can we talk?"

Holy hell, she wasn't sure she was ready to see him. And even if she was, she felt as if she should throw on a dress and some heels before she opened her door. "It's late."

"I know."

"I should go to bed. Maybe tomorrow."

There was a brief silence. "I have to go back tomorrow morning."

She frowned and glanced at the clock on her wall. "But it is tomorrow morning."

"I realize that. I have to go back in three hours."

"You came all the way up here for three hours?"

"Some things need to be said in person."

Stunned, she walked over and opened the door. Wow…he seemed so much taller in the suit, even though the top of his head was no higher off the ground than before.

"You don't look the same to me," she murmured. And it wasn't just because of his clothes.

"Can I come in?"

She stepped aside, and as he walked by, she looked him over. Even after having traveled five hundred miles, and in spite of the fact that it was now almost three in morning, he was as polished as the hood of a Ferrari.

But then maybe that was what expensive clothes got you. Perma-gleam.

As she closed the door, she resisted the urge to tug at her sweatshirt. Rearranging it wasn't going to change the fact that she'd paid nineteen dollars for it at Target. And anyway, she liked the darned thing. It was soft and comfortable…which was evidently more than could be said for what Sean had on. While he paced around, he yanked his tie loose as if he were dying to take it off.

He stopped and faced her. They both spoke at once.

"Sean—"

"Lizzie—"

She shook her head. "You first."

"No, what were you going to say?"

"Would you like something to drink?"

"I was wrong to think you were bilking my father. And I'm very sorry."

Lizzie's brows shot up. So much for social pleasantries and just as well. "I didn't use him, Sean."

"I know." He went over to the Venetian blinds, fingered them apart and peered outside. "I just couldn't figure out why you would be so close with him. Other than that."

"He was kind to me and he needed help." Censure creeped into her voice. "He had no one."

"Indeed." He dropped his hand and turned back to her. "Anyway, I'm honestly sorry."

"Apology accepted." Boy, he looked tired. "You know, you really could have said this over the phone."

"Assuming you'd have answered my call. And I wouldn't have blamed you if you didn't." He ran his hand down the length of his beautiful tie. "I should have told you about me earlier, but I liked the anonymity. I wanted to just be me with you."

"So you really thought I was a gold digger, huh?"

"Maybe."

"Definitely."

He shrugged. "Most of the women I've been with are fiscally minded. And not because they're in banking."

"Your poor choices, not my fault. Dear God, I don't want your money. Sure, I've got some problems with my job situation and my mother, but I wouldn't solve them by using you. I liked being with you."

He frowned. "Liked…past tense."

"Come on, Sean. You left and didn't look back this week. And besides, what do we have in common?"

His eyes traced over her face. "I thought of you the whole time. I wanted to call you, but the deal I'm working on is complex and at a critical—"

"People make time for what they want to do. They make the time." She shook her head and wrapped her arms around her waist. "It's okay, though. I mean—"

"I also didn't know what to say. I just didn't know how to tell you I missed you. I haven't missed anyone in a long time. I'm not used to it."

Lizzie's body stilled until her heart barely beat. The apology she expected. The revelation was a surprise.

"You mind if I sit down?" he said as he wrenched his tie off altogether and stuffed it in his jacket pocket.

"Ah, no…please do."

His big body sank into her sofa and he crossed his legs, ankle on knee. Stretching one of his arms out over the top of the cushions, he looked not just tired but depleted.

In the silence, she tried to see past the fancy suit and

the big-shot job and the net worth to the man she had been with before.

Because she'd really liked the person she'd watched playing Frisbee.

She truly had.

Chapter Ten

As Sean sat on the sofa, he had to hold on to the back of the damn thing to keep himself in place. He'd been fighting the urge to hug Lizzie since the moment she'd peaked out from between the blinds, and now that it looked as if she'd partially forgiven him, he wanted her against him so badly.

Plus she looked adorable in her baggy blue sweatshirt and those loose men's boxer shorts.

A surreptitious glance at her smooth legs had him tightening his grip on the couch. Oh, man, he really didn't trust himself to stay away from her. He was feeling the effects of a week of not sleeping on top of his manic rush to the airport, the hour-long flight and the drive into Southie.

So he was weak right now. Or rather, his hold on himself was weak.

What he wanted was to reconnect with her skin to skin and to hell with the talking. But he respected her too much to try and seduce her, and besides, it was clear she was wary of him, as well she might be. Hell, he was wary of himself. Nothing about this thing with her was making any sense to him, and when he felt off-kilter, he tended to get more aggressive, not less.

Letting his head go lax, he eased back into the cushions and eyed her from beneath his lids. She was pretty, her hair all disheveled, her face clean and a little shiny. She reminded him of things that were real, not pretension.

"You look exhausted," she said.

"I am."

"When does your plane leave?"

"Whenever I tell it to."

Her eyes dropped away. "Oh…yes, of course."

He waited for her to say something else. When she didn't, he realized he hadn't reached her far enough. His apology had been accepted, yes. But there was no going back.

So he should head out.

Sean sat up and put his hands on his knees, feeling as if there were an anvil on his chest. "Well, I—"

"Have you eaten?"

"Ah…no."

"Would you like to? Because I owe you one. You made me breakfast."

Okay…maybe there was a little light at the end of the tunnel. "I would love something. Thank you."

She nodded once and turned away.

"Lizzie?"

Her eyes bounced around the living room, avoiding his. "Yes?"

He wanted to keep pressing the apology stuff until she not only believed him but forgave him for having had so little faith in her.

"I don't care what it is. The breakfast, I mean. I'll love whatever you give me."

She nodded and turned away. As he watched her go, he let his head fall back again and he closed his eyes. Just for a moment.

He wasn't sure what woke him up or how long he'd been asleep, but it was still dark out when he came to. As he shifted and looked around, his neck was stiff and his jacket was wrinkled. There was a quilt around his legs as well as a plate with a sandwich on it and a glass of water on the table next to him.

He downed the water, ate the sandwich and went to find Lizzie.

The door to her bedroom was ajar and he pushed it open a little farther. Oh, man, just where he wanted her to be: curled on her side, her hair on her pillow, the room dim and cool.

He was such a bastard, he thought. Because he was going to get into that bed with her.

He quietly kicked off his wingtips and got out of his jacket then went over to the side he'd slept on before. As he lifted the covers, he eased his body in, but there was no way his two-hundred-and-ten-pound self wasn't making a dent in the mattress. As he got horizontal,

Lizzie was sucked into the hole he made, coming flush against him.

She was warm with sleep, a little ball of sumptuous ember, and he pulled her against his chest. As his head went down on the pillow, it found the crook of her fragrant neck.

He didn't mean to kiss her there. It just happened when she made a noise deep in her throat and undulated against him. As she arched, her skin met his lips.

It was a match to gasoline situation for them both.

They went body-to-body in a single surge, melding together through his clothes and hers. As he found her mouth, he kissed her deeply, taking what she offered even though he had no idea where they stood. The only thing he knew as they devoured each other was that his curious desperation for her was his undoing.

He broke away from her only long enough to split his shirt down the middle, and as the buttons flew, she took her own top off and shrugged out of her boxers.

He stopped with his hands on his belt and cursed. "I didn't bring any…"

"I got some in case you ever…um…we ever…"

His relief came out as a hoarse groan and he quickly ditched his trousers, tossing them to the floor as if they were trash.

"Where?" he groaned as he landed on top of her and pushed her legs apart with his own.

As she stretched out an arm to open a drawer on the bedside table, he latched onto her breast. There was a clatter as something hit the floor and then she was pressing a foil packet into his hand.

"I have no patience tonight," he warned against her nipple. Then he lifted his hips from hers and ripped the wrapper open with his teeth.

Her eyes were heated as they locked on to his body. "I don't want your patience."

"Good." He spit a piece of foil out, covered himself and then took her in a rush.

They both shouted and her nails scored his back as a climax rolled over her, through her. He absorbed the sensations of her grabbing on to him and then he let loose until he was heaving on top of her, riding her hard, driving them both into a frenzy.

Lizzie was mindless underneath Sean's rhythm, nothing but the sensations in her body. Just as he growled low in his throat and his body tensed from shoulder to thigh, she seized up again and arched into him. They shuddered together, his arms shooting around her and squeezing tight.

It was a while before either one of them could catch their breath and he rolled off her slowly as if he didn't want to leave. "You okay?"

She smiled at the hoarse sound of his voice. "Are you always going to ask that?"

"If things keep up like this, yes."

"I'm fine."

"Be right back."

As Sean disappeared into the bathroom, she lost her grin and the bed got cold fast.

What was she doing? This…whatever it was…with him was so awkward. Even though they were great

together in bed, she didn't know whether there could
be anything else between them.

She sat up and looked around for her T-shirt. She
found it just as he came in.

"Can I stay?" he asked as she pulled the thing over
her head.

Yanking her hair free of the collar, she said, "Sean…I
don't know. What just happened was probably a mistake."

As he put his hands on his hips, she had to fight to
ignore how astoundingly beautiful he was naked.

She cleared her throat. "I think you should go."

Because given that she was conflicted, if he stuck
around, she was liable to be swayed by his proximity.

Good Lord, who wouldn't be swayed by a man like
this?

For a moment, she thought he was going to argue,
but then he nodded and bent down to the floor. He
pulled his trousers on commando, picked up his boxers
and his shirt and jacket and went to the door.

"Mind if I call you?"

"Don't ask me that, Sean. Do it or don't."

His brows dropped down low. "Fair enough."

He turned away and didn't look back.

As his footsteps went down the hall, her heart felt
like a lead ball in her chest.

Just as she heard the front door open, something
made her spring out of bed and run for the living room.
She stopped herself in the hall, though.

Desperation was not good in situations like this.

Keeping herself in check, she watched him shut her

door then listened to him go up the stairs and settle directly above her.

He was sleeping on the couch again.

As she went back to her bed, she wondered why he did that. And was reminded of why a relationship would be so difficult with him.

It was hard to fall in love with someone who couldn't share himself with you.

In Sean's dream, the one that really got to him, the one that was the worst of the bunch, he was ten years old and coming home from dinner at a friend's house. It was winter and the snow was falling. His too-small boots were squeezing his toes until they were numb. His mittens had holes at the tips of the fingers and the pads of the thumbs. His jacket was thin and dirty.

But his stomach was full and that made all the difference. His school buddy, Butch O'Neal, had a mother who was a cook and a half. And as the O'Neals had five kids, one more mouth was no big deal.

Sean went over to their house a lot.

As he walked along in the dark, the snowbanks came up to his shoulders and he imagined himself on the ice planet Hoth from the *Star Wars* movies. He was Han Solo back from rescuing Luke…and Princess Leia was waiting at home for him.

He smiled, picturing himself as a hero.

Except then he came up to his house. All the lights were off on the top floor and the TV was flickering blue and green in the front window.

Lights off was a bad sign.

He looked at the downstairs unit. It was dark, as well, because the tenants had moved out a week ago. That always made things worse.

It happened a lot. Those first-floor people never stayed long. He had a feeling they didn't like the noises that came from upstairs and he could understand why. He didn't like the noises, either. He would have moved out if he could have.

Though his teeth were chattering, he hung around outside, packing snowballs and watching the TV do its thing in the living room. He wondered where his brothers were. He figured Mac would be at work still and Billy would be in their room in bed. Billy was always asleep if he was home. Didn't matter what time of the day it was, if he was there, you'd find him with his head under his pillow and the blankets up to his chin.

When Sean couldn't stand the cold any longer, he walked up the front steps and went to the door. He had to turn the knob a couple of times because his mittens were slippery from the snow and his hands were stiff.

And maybe because he would have given anything to have somewhere else to go.

He stepped into the foyer and was careful to be very quiet as he went up to his apartment. The higher he got on the stairs, the drier his mouth became until he was swallowing nothing at all and his tongue was like sandpaper.

He took off his right mitten and went for the doorknob. It was locked.

He closed his eyes and shivered. He knew why his father did this and it wasn't to keep out thieves. It was so Eddie O'Banyon would have to be inconvenienced

when his sons came home. So he would have to get out
of his chair and weave across the room. So he would
be justified in what came next.

Sean lifted his little hand and formed a loose, insub-
stantial fist. He knocked as quietly as he could, as if
maybe it would bother his father less.

Didn't work.

A monster opened the door. And a monster dragged
him inside. And a monster ripped his dirty snow jacket.

But before things got really bad, Mac came bursting
into the apartment, home just in time. Sean had some
impression of getting thrown in his room, not by his
father, but by his brother. And then his door clapped
shut.

As he landed in a heap, his face was throbbing to the
beat of his heart and his knees were weak and the food
that Mrs. O'Neal had made was a lead weight in his gut.

He started in with the dry heaves.

"W-w-wait! D-d-don't throw up on the r-r-rug!"
Billy stammered.

There was a scramble over by the desk and then a
wastepaper basket was shoved under Sean's face. Billy
held him off the floor as he threw up Mrs. O'Neal's
dinner and the only good thing about the retching was
that it drowned out the noises from the living room.

Except then the nausea passed and they heard everything.

"Oh God…" Sean whispered as a loud thump hit the
wall just outside their bedroom.

Billy started to cry.

The two of them ended up in Sean's bed with the

sheets pulled up over their heads. They trembled together as they listened. Eventually, it all went silent.

Sean waited for exactly one hour. He timed it, watching the alarm clock on the bureau, the one that got them up for school.

Then he shifted off the bed.

"Where are you g-g-going?" Billy whispered.

Sean didn't want his little brother to come. Didn't want Billy to see. "Go back to sleep."

"B-b-be careful."

"Shh."

Sean cracked open the door and winced as the thing creaked. Going utterly still, he waited while his heart pounded, and when nothing came at him, he slipped out into the hall. The TV was still on, still flickering, the glow throwing shadows as if things were coming at him.

There was something wet on the floor.

Sean was shaking as he went into his older brother's bedroom and he was careful as he shut the door behind him. Quiet. Had to stay quiet. He didn't want to wake the demon, although their father was likely passed out cold.

"Mac?" The room was dark and he couldn't see much, just the outline of the furniture. "Mac?"

There was a shuffling noise, as if someone had moved a leg or an arm.

With his eyes still adjusting, he went over to his brother's bed out of memory. But there was no one in it.

"Where are you?"

Another shuffle.

Sean tracked the sound over to the corner.

And that was where he found his fifteen-year-old brother, on the floor in a ball, hidden on the far side of his bureau.

"Mac, are you okay?" He went over and when he reached out, he felt something wet. He knew it wasn't tears. Mac never cried, no matter how bad it got. "Mac?"

"Go to bed." The voice was nothing but an exhausted whisper, more hoarse breath than words.

Sean patted his brother because it seemed like something their mom might have done. But Mac jerked away as if it hurt then groaned as if any kind of movement was a problem.

"Mac…I'm scared. What do I do?"

"What I told you. Go to bed."

"You're hurt."

"Go to bed."

Sean started to cry, and though he did his best to stop, the sniffles won. As his brother's hand landed on his shoulder, he was ashamed.

"Billy's wicked scared, right?" Mac said roughly.

"Yeah."

"So go take care of him. Go on."

"But you're—"

"If Dad finds you in here, we're all in trouble. *Go*."

That got Sean moving like nothing else could. He scooted back to his room, back to Billy. Who was indeed wicked scared.

"I d-d-don't want to l-l-live here anymore," Billy said.

"I'll take you away. I'll take you and Mac away."
Sean lay back down, closed his eyes and thought of Han
Solo the hero. Fearless and strong. Protector of the
weak. Champion. "I promise, Billy."

Sean sat up in a rush and nearly flipped himself off
the couch. He blinked hard and raised his arm to shield
his eyes. Light was spilling into the living room, all
bright and cheerful, but it registered as glare.

As he thought about the dream, his stomach rolled.
In the end, he hadn't been able to keep that promise to
Billy; he hadn't managed to get his brothers out. Time
had been their slow, disinterested savior, their age of
majority all that had rescued them. Mac, who'd taken
the brunt of the beatings, had been the last to leave,
staying until Billy was out then disappearing into the
army.

Never to be seen again, really.

Sean couldn't blame the guy for that. After years of
running interference, no wonder Mac had had it with
his younger brothers. He'd more than paid his dues.
Besides, Sean often wondered whether his brother
thought less of him and Billy. Mac had rarely cracked,
but Sean and Billy had. Often.

With his older brother on his mind, Sean checked his
watch and calculated what time it was on the other side
of the globe. Not that it would matter. Mac wouldn't
answer the number he'd left for calling. Never did.

Sean grabbed his BlackBerry, dialed what he'd been
given and laid down another message, all no pressure,
just-give-me-a-buzz-when-you-can. He figured he'd let

one more week go by and then he'd just tell the record-
ing that their father had died.

After he hung up, he showered and made some
phone calls to New York to keep his mind off Lizzie.
He wanted nothing more than to go down to her place,
and not just because he was rattled from his dream. He
was worried that they'd had their last night together and
the concern wasn't sitting well.

His instinct was to press her, but that wasn't fair. Best
thing was to give her a little space and pray that she
came around. Hell, he wasn't sure exactly what he
wanted out of a relationship with her. It wasn't as if he
had the capacity to fall in love with anyone. But he
knew that he wanted to see her again.

Maybe even *had* to see her again.

Man…he didn't enjoy feeling like this. Especially as
he couldn't seem to pull himself out of the emotions.

But at least work wasn't a problem this morning.
There was good news on the Condi-Foods deal. The
memorandum of understanding from the acquirers had
hit his offices at 4:00 a.m. for his review, and the share
price and interest payments had been adjusted to what
they'd agreed on. Which meant they had the bastards in
writing.

As soon as he got back to Manhattan this morning,
he was going to double check the documents then meet
with the board chair to give his go-ahead. It was going
to be big news on the Street, though the leaks were
already out there. The news outlets had started calling
his office.

Sean got dressed, throwing a polo shirt on under his

suit for the trip back because he'd shredded his button-down. He was just about to lock up when he heard the sound of a car engine turning over and wheezing out. There was a pause. Then the starter's whirring noise went off again only to fade after nothing caught.

He went over to the bay window and looked through the old lace curtains.

In the street down below, Lizzie got out of her Toyota and marched back into the duplex.

Sean descended the stairs at a clip and leaned into the open doorway of her apartment. "You need help?"

Lizzie was holding the phone to her ear and tapping her foot in frustration. Dressed in the loose scrubs of a nurse, her face was clean and shiny, her hair softly curling up as if it were only partially dry from a shower. She was frazzled, her mouth set with frustration, that foot going like the third hand on a watch, but she looked fantastic to him.

She lowered the receiver from her mouth. "My car does this sometimes. Just refuses to wake up."

"And you're late?"

"I wanted to get in early for my last day today. Boy, that starter motor has always had perfect timing. Perfectly *bad* timing."

"Can I drive you somewhere?"

"No, thanks. I'm on with the cab—" She cleared her throat and spoke into the phone. "Hi, I'd like a pickup at…"

As she talked with the taxi company, Sean stared at her, thinking he was the one who should drive her to work.

"I'm sorry, how long?" she said. "*Forty*-five minutes?"

"Let me take you," he cut in.

"I…ah—"

"Lizzie, I'll take you wherever you need to go. Let me do it."

Her eyes shifted to him. There was a pause. Then she said into the receiver, "Sorry, yes, I'm still here. But…ah, I don't need the cab. Thank you." She hung up. "You look like you're about to leave, though."

"I am. Right after I take you to work."

"I'm going to Roxbury."

"Then so am I."

"Okay…thank you. I just need to call the garage." She was quick and to the point with the mechanics, and after she hung up, she grabbed her purse and keys. "They're going to send a tow for it. They're used to me."

Damn it, he hated that her ride was unreliable. But as he followed her outside, he kept his yap shut. It wasn't as if she needed to hear that right now because she was no doubt thinking the same thing.

Without saying a word, they both paused on the shallow porch. The sun was a golden yellow, the sky a brilliant robin's-egg-blue, the trees as green as emeralds. It was as if the world had been colored by children's crayons.

"Beautiful day," he said.

"Yes." She looked around. "Like a cartoon almost. Reminds you of when you were young, doesn't it? So simple and clear and beautiful." She made an awkward sound. "Guess that's silly."

"Actually, it was just what I was thinking."

Her eyes shifted over, and for a split second, the

connection was there between them again, as invisible as the air that separated them, but as warm and real as the sunshine on their faces.

"Lizzie," he breathed.

"We...better go." Except she didn't look away. And neither did he.

Sean leaned down and put his lips on hers. There was so much he wanted to say, but he kept it simple and clear as the day. "I'm glad I'm taking you to work."

He took her hand and they walked to the rental in silence. After he opened her door for her, he waited until she was settled, then went around to the driver's side.

As they headed off for Roxbury, she said, "I wanted to let you to know I'm moving out."

Sean's hands cranked down hard on the wheel and he had to force them to relax. "You don't have to."

"I want to leave."

"Why?" Even though he knew.

"Too many memories." Then she quickly added, "Besides, if I end up working downtown during the day, it would be better if I lived closer to a T-stop."

He frowned. "How is the job search going?"

"It's going. Just started, really."

He glanced across the seat. Her eyes were trained out the side window, but they were unfocused, as if she were reviewing her situation in her head.

Sean thought about her mother. Her broken-down car. The fact that she was working nights in a rough part of town.

"Listen, you can forget about the rent," he said. "I mean, until I sell the place."

She looked at him in surprise then shook her head. "Oh, no. That's okay. I'll be fine, but thanks."

Man… First time he could remember a woman turning him down for money. But then Lizzie wasn't fitting the pattern in any manner, was she?

"Well, the offer stands," he said. God, he was a bastard to have ever doubted her for a moment. No way she'd been after his father for cash. No. Way.

After hitting all the red lights in Boston and getting slowed up by some sewer work, they eventually made it to Roxbury.

"It's on the next block." Lizzie pointed out the windshield. "Right here."

The community health center was set up in a two-story building constructed of concrete bricks and marked with windows that had chicken wire in the glass. But it wasn't dour. There were flowers in pots in front of the door and a lovely maple on the front lawn. And everything was neat as a pin: the grass between the sidewalk and the foundation was trimmed, and the juniper bushes were clipped nice and tight and the entryway was swept clean. Sun glinted off the front doors and made the brass sign that read Roxbury Community Health Initiative glow.

There were some people milling around, two of whom were in white coats and obviously doctors or nurses. The others seemed like a family: the woman with a baby in her arms and a toddler latched onto one leg, the man with a five-year-old up on his shoulders.

"Nice-looking place," Sean said.

"It is. The people who work here are so committed.

And the patients we treat are very special. I've been lucky to be a part of it."

"Even with the cuts in funding, it'll still stay open, right?"

"The question is for how long. We're—*they're* close to the bone already, working with equipment that needs to be upgraded in a facility that's really too small. The thing that scares me is, I don't know what this community would do without these services. So many folks aren't able to get downtown to the big medical centers, either because they don't have the money to travel that far or there are child-care issues or they can't take off the time from work to spend all afternoon in a doctor's office that's miles away." She shook her head and put her hand on the door. "Anyway…thanks for the ride."

"Wait, how long have you worked here?"

"Two years." Her eyes shifted back to the center. "Two years and two months. Like I said, I was right out of nursing school when I came onboard. Hard to believe it's my last day. I'm going to miss this place."

As Lizzie got out, the folks around the front door called her by name and she greeted them as one would friends, not patients or colleagues.

She leaned down into the rental car. "Thanks again, Sean."

"Lizzie?"

"Yes?"

"When do you get off?"

"Late today because they're throwing me a goodbye party. So not until sevenish. Why?"

"Just wondering. Take care."

Chapter Eleven

"So who *was* he, Lizzie?"

As the little conference room went silent, Lizzie looked up from her slice of We'll Miss You cake. The question had been popped by one of the other nurses, and with all the attention on her, Lizzie figured she had few options for response: Just a friend. No one special. Son of her landlord.

Or she could go with the truth: Wall Street tycoon with whom she'd had a very short-lived affair. Who was kind of still hanging around.

Ugh.

"Who are we talking about?" someone else asked.

"The guy who dropped off Lizzie today. The very handsome guy."

Keep it simple, stupid, Lizzie thought. "He's just a friend. My car died again."

"Well, from what I saw," a third person cut in, "a friend like him would be good to have."

Everyone smiled at her and piled on with good-natured ribbing. Which naturally caused Lizzie to turn as red as a stop sign.

Thank heavens the conversation was cut off by Denisha. The hollow sound of a plastic fork tapping on a plastic cup shifted the focus to the director. "I just want to take a minute to thank Lizzie for everything she's done."

"Hear! Hear!" came the chorus.

As people said a lot of really nice things, Lizzie looked down and pushed a wedge of frosting around her plate. She couldn't meet the eyes of her colleagues. Not with the tears that were threatening to spill at any minute.

"Lizzie?" Denisha said. "We have something for you."

Lizzie glanced up. "Really, that's not—"

The director held out an envelope. "This is for you."

Lizzie put her little plate down and took it. After working the flap free, she pulled out a homemade card with…oh, God…hundreds of signatures on it: patients and colleagues and the cleaning staff and the lawn men she'd helped with the flowers and the UPS guy and the medical reps who visited regularly.

She blinked fast so that only one tear escaped and hit the card. "You have no idea…what this means to me." She put her present up to her chest as if she could embrace at once all the people who had cared enough to sign it. "I will miss you so much."

A group hug bloomed all around her, people sniffling and smiling and holding on.

It was a sweet, sweet moment, proving that one person could make a difference to others. And it reminded her of why she'd become a nurse. There was great satisfaction in being a part of something like this, part of a place that cared about a community and healed the ill and infirm. She only hoped she could find something half as fulfilling somewhere else.

When the party broke up, she tidied the conference room with the others, grabbed her purse and her card of signatures and went out to the front desk to call a cab.

She was dialing when one of the nurses said, "He's back."

Lizzie didn't pay much attention as her call was answered by the taxi company. "Hi, I'd like a cab—"

"You don't need one, Lizzie. Your friend's back. And…wow is all I can say."

Lizzie frowned then leaned over the desk and looked out the double doors. A rental car was parked in front and Sean was lounging against the side of it, facing the community center. Wearing jeans and a New England Patriots T-shirt, he looked sexy as hell with his thick arms crossed over his chest and his sunglasses on.

Lizzie mumbled something to the cab folks, put the phone down and walked over to the door. "He isn't supposed to be here."

"Honey, man like that shows up for you, I'd say he's supposed to be here. And that you won the lottery."

As Sean lifted his hand and waved to her, she realized she was just staring at him like an idiot.

Shaking herself into focus, she gave a quick hug to her colleague then gathered her things and pushed open the door. The evening was a balmy benediction as she stepped outside.

"Um…I thought you were going back to New York."

"I did. Flew in for the meeting I had and came back. I figured I'd stop by here on the way home from Logan. How's your car?"

"Still getting worked on. I…I can't believe you came back."

"I have an ulterior motive."

She swallowed. "You do?"

"Yeah, can you give me a tour?" He nodded at the center. "Or is it too late at night?"

He wanted to see the center? "Ah…of course. The director is still here. I can introduce you to her and she can—"

"No, I want you to take me around. I want to see it through your eyes."

"Okay. But…Sean, why?"

"I'm always interested in businesses, but in this case, I might be able to help. The governor of this fine state happens to have been my college roommate and I'm not above hard-core lobbying for the right cause."

As Sean smiled, she found herself returning the expression. And tried not to let her heart soar. "Anything you could do would be appreciated, but I don't think it's the governor, actually. The legislature has been blocking his bid to get more funding to us. That's where the bottleneck is."

"Well, I'm glad to know your fine governor is

already onboard. It will make things so much easier on him when I start hammering him about your state-house." Sean stepped out of the car. "Shall we?"

Lizzie took him inside and led the way to Denisha's office so they could make sure the tour was okay. When Denisha gave her approval, Lizzie showed Sean around the exam rooms and talked to him about some of the patients they treated.

On the way to the lab facilities, she stopped in the doorway of the radiology room. "We really need better equipment. We have to send some patients out to other facilities to get certain films done and that is a hassle for them—more expensive, too. The advantage to us being in the community is that folks don't have to travel when they're sick. We're right here. And because we're user-friendly, important health screens for breast cancer and diabetes and high blood pressure are more likely to be conducted because patients adhere to their yearly checkups more often. If this center closes, or has to outsource too much, I really worry about the people we serve."

Sean frowned. "How tight is your budget?"

"Reimbursements from Medicaid and Medicare are not what they once were and our expenses are always higher so it's a thousand small cuts. If this continues, we're not going to be able to meet the standard of patient care because we'll be too understaffed and technologically compromised. And we aren't the only clinic in this situation. There are a number of facilities just like this, serving at-risk populations as we do. I mean…they."

Sean shook his head as the two of them came back

to the front desk. "Does this place have an endowment? I mean, what kind of philanthropic support do you get?"

"Some. Not enough. And no, we don't have an endowment."

Denisha came out of her office. "Did you enjoy your tour?"

Sean offered his hand and they shook. "You're doing really wonderful work here."

"Thanks." Denisha glanced over. "And Lizzie is one of our best. We're really going to miss her."

Lizzie looked away, not wanting to get emotional in front of Sean. "But I'm going to volunteer. So I'll be back."

"Good."

A few more things were said, but Lizzie wasn't really following. She was too busy looking at the crayon drawings that some of the kids had done while in the waiting room. The white papers with rainbow marks were taped up on the hallway's wall, a quilt of exuberance and life drawn by the community's future leaders.

"Lizzie? You ready?" Sean said.

"Yes." Though she wasn't.

She hugged Denisha tightly, but didn't lose it, and was proud of herself for getting to the car without a lot of drama.

Sean opened the passenger-side door for her. "You got any plans tonight?"

"I'm moonlighting."

"Okay, I'll be your taxi."

"Really, Sean, you've already done too much.

Besides, I have the home trip covered. I'm catching a ride back with a friend of mine who's pulling a double shift tonight."

"Then at least let me take you there, okay?"

As he shut the door and walked around the hood of the car, she watched him move. All that lithe male grace was something to see and she couldn't believe she'd been with him. Naked. In her bed.

She was so in trouble with this man.

"Why are you doing this?" she blurted as he got behind the wheel. "I mean…going to all this effort?"

He turned the key in the ignition and glanced at her as the engine flared to life. His deep-set hazel eyes were so serious that she was taken aback.

"You said it best. People make time for what they want. And I want you." Sean hit the gas and pulled away from the curb, resuming a more normal expression. "So when do you go to work? You want dinner?"

"Are you seeing anyone else?" she blurted. "I mean, down in the city?"

He shook his head. "It's just you. Only you, Lizzie."

Oh crap. That was so the right answer.

She rubbed her temples, thinking that this felt a lot like a relationship. It really did. Part of her wanted to fight falling into it. Part of her couldn't stop herself.

"I—ah, I usually eat something at the hospital around midnight. But there isn't time. I'm due in at eight."

"Okay, so are you free tomorrow night? My brother's in town for a preseason game. You want to come with me? We usually go out for a bite after he plays."

She loved football. "I don't know."

As Sean looked back over at her, his eyes were serious again. "Yeah, you do. But you don't trust me. Look, I'm hoping that we can spend some time together so that maybe…yeah, maybe you'll get to trusting me again."

"Sean, I'm not interested in getting my heart broken."

"Then we have something in common. I'm not interested in breaking your heart. I made a mistake. I'm sorry. And I want to keep seeing you."

She was about to ask him why when she realized that sounded pathetic. She was a good person. A smart person. She might not have millions in the bank or a flashy lifestyle, but that didn't mean she wasn't worthy of him.

"So what do you say, Lizzie? Little football in the afternoon. Little bite afterward. You know, real regular date stuff."

She took a deep breath. "Okay. It sounds…great."

He reached across the seat and took her hand. Then melted her by bringing it to his lips and whispering, "Thank you for the second chance."

When they got back to the duplex, Sean opened her door for her then hung back against one of the jambs as she went inside.

Man, he was tired.

He'd killed himself to get back to Boston tonight in time to pick her up and that was on top of a long day. After he'd raced down to Manhattan this morning, he'd had the meeting with the Condi-Foods board chair, a video conference conducted with investors in Tokyo and a drawn-out argument with one of his partners. Then he'd hightailed it back here.

The whole time he'd been en route, whether in limos or on the plane, he'd been working on his laptop, processing the hundreds of details and decisions that went along with a complex acquisition like Condi-Foods. When he'd waited for Lizzie at the health center, he'd made an effort to appear casual so she didn't feel pressured or stalked, but it had cost him a lot to haul ass up and down the coast.

Why had he made the effort? He'd had to come back to her. He'd made the time.

"I won't be long," Lizzie said as she went over to her computer and checked her e-mail.

"Don't rush on my account." When she made a frustrated sound, he asked, "What's the matter?"

"Oh, nothing." She blew out her breath. "Well, actually, I applied for four jobs last night. Two have already been filled, one was mis-listed and another I've been told I'm overqualified for. Usually there are a lot of nursing jobs available, but the class that graduated over this summer has taken some of the opportunities I could have used. But, whatever. At least I have the night work at the emergency department. And I put in some other applications on my lunch break today. Maybe one of them will come through…." She let the sentence drift, then headed off down the hall. "I'll be right back."

As Sean heard the shower come on, he imagined what she looked like, taking off her scrubs, stepping under the warm water, soaping up her body. He leaned his head back against the jamb and stared at the ceiling.

Wanting a specific woman was a new experience, but it was very clear that he had a case of the desperates for Lizzie. His blood was running red-hot again and the only thing that was going to put out the fire was her.

His BlackBerry went off, which was a relief. With any luck, he'd get sufficiently distracted so that what was doing behind his fly wouldn't show by the time Lizzie came back out.

After checking caller ID, he put his phone to his ear. "Mick, what's the news?"

"Congratulations, buddy, you did it. The Condi-Foods board signed off on the deal. You're going to get the formal call in about ten minutes. Holy hell, biggest transaction on the books this year and it's all you."

Sean heard the shower turn off. "That's great news, my man."

Mick laughed. "You're always so tight about these things. Most guys I know would be hopping around the room and breaking out the Cohibas."

"Lot of work to get to the finish line even with the board's approval." As doors were open and shut down the hall, he imagined Lizzie walking around in a towel. "It's not over yet."

"We need to celebrate anyway. How long are you going to be up there in Beantown?"

"I'll come back on Sunday night."

"Your father's place almost boxed up?"

"Haven't started yet."

There was a pause. "So what's been going on in Boston?"

"Nothing."

"You're spending a lot of time there for someone who still has packing to do."

Lizzie's voice carried down the hall. "Almost ready, Sean."

"Who's that?" Mick demanded.

"I've got to go, buddy."

"The hell you do. You seeing someone up there?"

"Ah...kind of." Assuming she'd have him.

The laugh that came across the line was a low, very masculine *gotcha*. And it took Sean back to a similar conversation he once had with a friend. Yeah, except back then with Gray Bennett, his buddy had been the one falling for a woman. And Sean had been the guy laughing.

Guess this was payback.

"So who is she, SOB?"

"You don't know her."

"Then you need to bring her to New York. I want to meet the woman who's gotten you to travel *to* her."

Lizzie walked in, dressed in a fresh pair of scrubs. "I'm ready—oh, sorry."

As she made like she was going to duck out of the room, he shook his head to stop her. "Look, I've got to go, Mick. I'll call you later." As he hung up without waiting for a response, an odd sinking sensation washed over him. Would she ever come to New York? he wondered. "So where we headed?"

"Boston Medical Center." She frowned and tilted her head to one side. "Hey, your right eye is twitching. Are you okay?"

He rubbed at the thing, annoyed by the way it was making his vision flicker. "Yeah, just fine. Actually, I got some great news from work."

"Good." Her stare surveyed him in what suddenly seemed like a professional manner.

He brought his hand up again and tried to get his eyelid to quit the disco routine.

"Sean, when was the last time you slept for more than a few hours?"

He had to smile. "Probably back when I was in college. That was basically the only time I slept well. But it's no big—"

Sean stopped breathing and blinked hard. Then scrubbed both his eyes. As he looked at Lizzie, half of her was gone, dissolved in a shimmering halo.

"Crap."

"Sean?"

"I'm having a migraine."

"Have you gotten them before?"

"Once or twice."

"Do you have medication?"

"No, because they don't come frequently enough. I think you'd better call a taxi because I can't drive right now. Oh, man… This is going to be a big one."

When Lizzie got home at 4:00 a.m., she opened the door to her apartment quietly and snuck in. The place was dead dark and dead silent.

Carefully putting her keys and purse on a table, she kicked off her shoes and padded down the hall. She put her head through her bedroom door and was disappointed when she saw through the dimness that her bed was empty.

Before she'd left for work, she'd pushed Sean between her sheets and closed the blinds and the curtains and told him to stay put. Clearly, though, he'd gone upstairs at some point.

Which meant she was going to go check on him. She wanted to see how he was doing and give him some of the over-the-counter medicine she'd picked up at the hospital.

Before she went up, she headed for the bathroom and flipped on the overhead—

Lizzie froze.

Sean was on the tile, curled up next to her toilet, having obviously spent some time throwing up. Had he passed out? she thought with panic.

A moan came up from the floor. "Lights off. Please."

She quickly hit the switch, and as blackness returned, he let out a ragged breath.

Kneeling by him, she whispered, "I have something for you to take if you'd like. Excedrin Migraine. It works very well or so I've heard."

His voice was reedy, nothing like the deep bass she was used to. "Don't think I could hold anything down."

"You want to go back to the bed?"

"Not yet."

"Do you need to go to the ER?"

"No."

She left and came back with a pillow and a blanket. Then she did the kindest thing she could for him: she left him alone.

After using the hall bath, she got into bed and stared

at the ceiling. Stress was a classic trigger for migraines and she was willing to bet his father's death coupled with whatever news had come from New York, even though it had been positive, had been what did it. All that travel couldn't have helped, either.

She thought of him lying in a ball on the floor. It was difficult to imagine someone as powerful as him being so fragile, but that was illness for you. As a nurse, she'd seen it so many times. Pain was the great equalizer, capable of stripping the crowns from kings.

She hated that Sean was hurting. And wished there was more she could do for him. Poor man...

She must have fallen asleep because sometime later the mattress wiggled. "Sean? How are you feeling?"

"Bad. Stomach has settled down though."

"Can I give you the meds?"

"Yeah."

She got the bottle, gave him two white pills with some water, and then lay back down beside him. As she turned to him, his hand came fishing through the sheets and the blankets and found hers. When he squeezed, she squeezed back.

"I'm right here if you need me," she said softly.

"Thanks." There was a stretch of silence. "I think I need you."

"You want something to eat? Drink?"

"No. I just...think I need you." He exhaled and fell silent.

She looked at the ceiling...and against her better judgment, beamed in the dark.

Chapter Twelve

"Could you please call my brother?"

It was late the next morning and Lizzie was standing over her bed, hands on her hips, clinical eye on Sean.

She ignored his request. "Have you ever had one that's lasted this long?"

"Yeah. It's been a decade, but yeah."

Boy, Sean was the color of kindergarten paste...except for the smudges of black under his eyes. His brows were cranked together, his breathing shallow. His big body was so still, it was obvious the slightest movement caused the headache to get worse. Still, he didn't seem to be in any medical danger. He was just miserable.

"So can you call Billy for me?" he asked. "I'm going

nowhere this afternoon. He'll also know how to get hold of Mick."

"How do I get in touch with your brother?"

"I'll give you his number."

She memorized the digits as he recited them. "You want anything?"

He managed to say the word *no* without moving his lips at all. Then tacked on, "Wait, my duffel bag from the car would be great. Has my toothbrush in it."

"Be right back."

After she got the bag and put it just inside her room, she shut the door and headed for the phone in the living room. While dialing his brother's number, she held her breath. She'd never spoken to a pro football player before.

The voice that answered was a low drawl. "Yeah?"

"Is this Billy O'Banyon?"

"Depends. Who are you and how did you get this number?"

Whoa. Evidently, linebackers had nice voices. "Assuming you are him, your brother Sean gave it to me."

There was a pause. Then the voice got sharp. "Is he okay?"

"He has a migraine. Bad one. He asked me to tell you that he won't be able to come to the game today."

"Oh, hell. Considering all that's been going on, I should have known one was coming. Where is he?"

"At your house."

"My house? Which one?" As if he had so many he couldn't keep track.

"Um…your father's house, I guess. In South Boston."

The man's tone turned incredulous. "He's still staying *there?*"

"Yes."

"Okay. Wow." There was another pause. "Tell him I'll stop over after the game."

"I'll pass on the message. Oh, and he wanted you to call Mick and let him know what's going on."

"Yeah, okay. Wait, who are you?"

"I live in the apartment below. I'm kind of taking care of him. My name's Lizzie Bond."

"Well, I appreciate your making the effort, especially because I'll bet you've got to tie him down to keep him still. That brother of mine never slows up."

"Well, he's slowed up now. Has been since last night."

"Poor bastard. How bad is he?"

"You can see for yourself. When you come by, just knock on the downstairs door. I'll be here, and considering how he's faring, so will he."

"I'll do that. And thanks again for watching over him."

As she hung up, she heard a noise from the bedroom and went down the hall. Sean was writhing on the bed, his big body twisting in the sheets, his brows drawn tight. He made a noise deep in his throat, a kind of strangled protest, then shook his head back and forth on the pillow.

She went over and touched his shoulder. "Sean?"

He woke up on a full recoil, his hands shielding his face as if he were about to be struck. In a voice that didn't sound like his at all, he said, "Please...no."

They'd done this before. The night of the storm.

"Sean?" she said gently, though she was thoroughly creeped out and worried about him. "Wake up. You're just dreaming."

"Mac?"

She frowned. "No, it's me. Lizzie."

He blinked a number of times, then sank back down into the pillows and closed his eyes. "Lizzie? Oh…yeah…yeah, I know. Sorry."

She stayed over the bed, the sound of his voice ringing in her mind. Mac was his other brother, right? And what had he been so afraid of? She had a feeling the dream was a repeater.

"Sean?" When he made an affirming noise, she said, "I'm going to go out for a little while, if you're okay?"

"I should probably leave, too. Not fair. Take up all your space." He started to push himself up, moving slowly as if he had an unbalanced load on his neck. Or maybe a ticking bomb.

"No, Sean. I want you to stay." The way he collapsed back down told her just how weak he was. "Listen, I have my cell with me and I've left the number by the phone, okay?"

"Don't want you to have to nurse me. 'Nough of that on your day job."

"I don't mind at all." She truly didn't. Although she was sorry he felt bad, she was glad he was in her bed, his hair dark against her pillows, his heavy shoulders filling out her blankets and covers. In her room, between her sheets, he was safe and she could care for him and he would be far more comfortable than upstairs on that couch he insisted on using.

"Thank you," he said in a garbled voice. "Once again."

Before she left, she had a consuming urge to kiss him on the forehead, but she resisted. "I'll be back."

She went out the front door a couple of minutes later and walked the long distance to the nearest T-stop. In the back pocket of her jeans was a list of open houses for apartments in Southie, Charlestown and Cambridge. She figured it was going to take a while to see them all.

She was right. And the prospects were bleak.

After three hours of hoofing it up and down stairs and taking the T around, she had a sense of what she could afford and it was not a lot. Prices had skyrocketed in the two years since she'd last been looking, and for what she was paying now, her only options were cramped studios in buildings that were kind of run down. Her only other choice was to look even farther out of Boston proper, to Watertown, for instance, but then getting to work would be more of a hassle.

On her way back home on the T, she called the service station and had to curse to herself. Her car was going to need a thousand dollars' worth of work. Evidently, it wasn't just the starter this time.

As the T trundled along and sank underground, she looked out and saw nothing but a rhythmic pattern of tunnel lights, some of which had burned out.

She really needed one of those job applications to come through. Fast.

For Sean, the migraine's pain started to recede about 250 years after it had started. Or maybe it was twenty-five minutes. Hard to tell. Time had warped, becoming like cloth that was bunched up and wrinkled. Maybe if he made an effort he could smooth it out and count the hours. But he really didn't care that much.

He rolled over onto his side and cracked an eyelid.

He was still in Lizzie's bed. Hell, he'd taken it over, lying in the middle as if he owned the damn thing. Man, bad enough to have been sick in front of her, but to have all but kicked her out of her own room? That was just awful.

He gingerly pushed himself onto his elbows and gave his head a moment to adjust to the altitude. Then he looked at the clock. It said nine and he was pretty sure that was nine at night. Yeah…no slits of sunlight through the drapes. Definitely nighttime.

He moved himself to the side of the bed slowly, feeling as if there were an anvil on the left side of his head. Still, the dull pain was a big improvement over the ax blade that had been there before.

As his feet hit the floor, he thought, okay, he could handle upright. And it was time to plug back into the real world. He needed to call Mick and get a status report on Condi-Foods. Had to check in with his office—

Whoa. The mere thought of doing either of those things brought the ax back. As his head started to pound again, he thought maybe he and his BlackBerry would stay estranged for a little longer.

Throwing the thoughts of work out the window, he concentrated on getting to the bedroom door in one piece. When that mission was accomplished, he opened the thing and followed the muted tapping of computer keys out to the living room.

"Hi."

Lizzie twisted around in the armchair by the window. "Hello!"

"I think I'm back in the land of the living."

"So you are. How's the head?"

"Still attached. Not real clear on whether that's a good thing, but at least I'm vertical."

"Good. Would you like something to eat?"

"I was thinking I'd get out of your hair, actually."

"Oh. Well, you weren't really in it. You've been a very quiet patient."

He pointed over his shoulder with his thumb. "I'm going to strip the bed. You got fresh sheets?"

"Don't worry about that. Besides, you look like you're about to fall over."

"I'm okay. Can't wait to have a shower though."

"Take one here if you want."

"No, thanks. I've intruded enough." With his energy already flagging, he glanced at the front door and wondered how he was going to make it to the second floor. But that wasn't what was really on his mind. "Ah hell, Lizzie, I've ruined your weekend."

"Are you kidding me? I wouldn't have done anything differently." She nodded at the computer. "Right now I'm all about the job search."

"Find anything?"

She shrugged. "A few. By the way, your brother said he was coming by, but I don't know how late."

Sean stopped breathing. "Here? He's coming *here?*"

"Yes." Lizzie frowned. "Is that bad? He's worried about you."

"No. It's just—" Sean cut himself off, thinking that if Billy was coming over, he didn't want his brother going upstairs. "You know what? I think I will shower down here, if you don't mind. And if he comes, would you feel comfortable just letting him in? He's a good guy. He only looks like a thug."

"Of course. Wait, what exactly does he look like? I don't watch football on TV."

"He's six-five, about 260 pounds. His hair's blond like my mother's was and he's got a jaw like a slab of rock."

"Sounds handsome."

In a flash, a good old-fashioned shot of jealous-for-no-damned-good-reason went through Sean's chest. *Handsome?*

"Ah, yeah, I guess he is," Sean muttered. Actually, his brother was a total looker and women always loved the guy. The bastard.

"Well, I'll watch out for him."

Sean nodded and headed for the bathroom, hoping to get in and out of it fast. And not just because he didn't want to keep his little brother waiting.

There was no reason to have Billy working out his charm on Lizzie.

Within moments of the shower starting, Lizzie heard the house's front doorbell ring.

She got up and went to the blinds. *Whoa...* There was a Greek god out on the porch: Billy O'Banyon just about defined jock handsome in his blue jeans and his white muscle shirt and his blond hair.

Yeah…wow. Check out those tattooed biceps.

Although it was funny. In spite of his obvious attributes, he couldn't hold a candle to Sean in her eyes.

She went out into the hall and opened the duplex's front door. "Hi, you must be Billy?"

The Adonis smiled, showing a row of white, even teeth. "I am. And you're Lizzie?" As she nodded, he stuck out his hand. "Nice to meet you. How's the patient?"

"Up and around. In the shower, actually." She stepped back and swept her arm toward her apartment. "He'll be right out."

When Billy stepped into the hallway, his demeanor changed completely. As his eyes drifted up the stairs, his face and his body stiffened, his charisma draining out of him.

He didn't move. Just stood there fixated.

"Um…he's in my shower," she prompted quietly.

"W-w-w-w." Billy shook his head. "I mean, what?"

"Sean… He's in my place."

"Oh. Yeah." Billy's eyes didn't leave the stairs. "H-how." More with the head shaking, as if he was trying to unstick his mouth. "H-h-how… *Damn* it, how is he?"

"Better. Much better."

"Good." Billy's massive chest expanded and then he looked at her. All at once, his face settled into a flashing smile that had about as much depth as water spilled on a counter. "I'm glad to hear it. He give you much trouble?"

"No." As Billy went into her apartment, she asked, "Would you like something to drink?"

"No, I hydrated before I came, but thanks." He looked around. "Nice place. Been here long?"

"Two years."

"Nice."

Standard social conversation, she thought, and she appreciated him making the effort, but she wished she could ask his what was wrong. The man who was standing in her living room was not the guy she'd opened the door to.

Down the hall, the shower shut off and there was the sound of a towel flapping around.

"Yo, Sean," Billy called out. "How you be?"

The door to the bathroom opened and Sean stuck his head out. His hair was sticking straight up like un-mowed grass and there was water dripping off his nose.

He looked fantastic. Until she got a gander at his eyes. They were locked on his brother and clearly worried.

"You okay?" Sean asked. Even though he'd been the one down for the count with that headache.

Billy nodded. "Y-y-yeah."

"Stay down here. You don't go up the stairs, okay?"

Billy nodded again as if he preferred not to trust his voice.

As Sean shut the door, there was an awkward silence.

Then Billy looked up to the ceiling. "You know my father at all?"

"Yes. We were friends."

His eyes shot to hers. As if he'd never expected to hear that word associated with the man. "Really. Huh. What was he like? As a friend?"

"He was good to me. I was grateful I knew him."

"Really. Huh." Same words, same inflection. As if his brain was multiprocessing and that was just what happened to spit out to fill conversational space. "He treat you good?"

"Yes."

"Really."

She waited for the *huh,* but it didn't come. "He looked after me in a way."

"Funny, I always thought he didn't care about people. Well, except for my mother. He loved her. But then she died and he changed. Everything changed. Forever."

The haunted quality of this big, beautiful man's voice made chills go up her spine. And the eerie feeling made her think of something Mr. O'Banyon had said once. It had been New Year's Eve and she'd been talking to him about regrets. He'd said he had none. What he had were things he could never atone for. Regrets... Regrets didn't go far enough.

She'd thought it was an odd way to put things, but he'd changed the subject and it had never come up again. Now, she looked back on that conversation and felt uneasy.

Billy brought his hand up to his chin. "Sometimes... Sometimes change isn't good, you know?"

She let the comment stand, because she was well aware he wasn't actually addressing her.

When a growling sound broke the silence, she frowned. Then realized it was Billy's stomach.

"Are you hungry?" she asked.

He looked down at his body as if surprised. "Yeah…I am."

"Come on, I was just about to make myself something to eat."

Chapter Thirteen

As Sean sat at his family's old table in Lizzie's kitchen, he had to give his brother credit. Billy was keeping it together, appearing to be what he was most of the time: a charmer of a guy with great people skills and a lot of bawdy stories.

But Sean knew the truth, knew how much it was costing his brother to be here. Billy had said he'd never come back to the duplex and it was clear the specter of what had happened upstairs was prowling around in the guy's head. Billy's eyes kept lifting to the ceiling as if he could see through the plaster and the Sheetrock and the framing boards into the past.

He was making an effort to keep tight, though, and Lizzie seemed to be having a great time as the two of them cooked then put dinner on the table. Man, it was a perfect summer meal. The hamburgers were stacked with juicy beef-steak tomatoes that spilled out of the bun as you bit down. The corn was sweet and tender. The lemonade was perfect and very chilly.

Except he didn't enjoy it as much as he could have. While they ate, he tried to get lost in the talk and the food, but it was tough. Even though he was in that post-migraine float zone where everything had soft edges, he kept thinking about Billy.

By the time a bag of oatmeal cookies was passed around, he was feeling the strain in his head.

After Billy told a real barn-burner of a story and Lizzie laughed so hard she was gasping for air, Sean's brother checked his sports watch. "I've got an early PT session tomorrow so unfortunately I have to take off soon." He got to his feet and picked up his plate as well as Lizzie's. "This has been great. Would love to do it again soon."

Lizzie grinned at him. "Yeah, well, I'd love to hear more stories from the locker room."

"I *knew* you were my kind of girl." The faux-leer Billy shot over his shoulder somehow managed to be both outrageous and respectful at the same time.

Which meant Sean didn't have to snap his brother's chain. Too hard. "Forget it, Billy, she's out of your league."

"I know. Too smart." Billy smiled at Lizzie. "You'd have to be smart to get through nursing school, right?"

"It helps," she said, winking at him.

Sean stood up. "I'll walk you to your car."

"Great." As Lizzie rose from the table, as well, Billy

stuck his hand out at her. "I'd hug you but I think my brother would hurt me."

"No, he wouldn't," she said.

Lizzie stretched up onto her toes and threw her arms around Billy. He was so big, she looked as if she were embracing the hood of a car, her reach not long enough by half. In response, Billy handled her gently, the way he did with all women. As a man who knew his strength, he was always careful around those more fragile than him.

Which was pretty much everyone on the planet.

"Okay, you can stop that," Sean said, putting his hand on Billy's shoulder and pulling back with a little tug.

Billy let go and wagged his eyebrows at Lizzie. "See. Told you."

She batted his tattooed bicep. "You know Sean's just kidding."

Yeah, the hell he was. "Come on, big man. Out."

As Billy laughed, Sean frog-marched him to the apartment's door, but they both got serious as he opened the thing. Stepping out into the foyer, he deliberately stood in the way of the staircase, trying to block as much of it as he could with his body.

Billy's eyes went up to the top landing and his mouth got grim.

Sean shook his head. "Come on, Billy. Let's go."

They went out of the house in silence and stayed that way while walking over to Billy's custom-rigged Denali.

"I didn't want you to come here," Sean said.

"Couldn't stay away forever."

"Yeah, you could have. And I'd have preferred that."

Billy's face tilted upward as he looked to the second-floor apartment. "What's it like in there?"

"Same. Exactly the same."

"Freak you out?"

"Yeah."

"You need help packing?"

"No." Not from his little brother, at any rate.

Billy rubbed his square jaw. "Did you see him dead?"

"Yeah."

"What did he look like?"

"Older. But like that damned apartment, the same."

There was a long period of quiet.

Down at the end of the street, a car turned onto the road. Its engine was a muted drone that got louder as it approached, then faded after it went by.

"You heard from Mac yet?" Billy asked.

"I left him another message a couple of days ago. Next time I'm just going to tell the voice mail."

"Wish he'd call."

"Me, too."

Billy leaned back against the SUV and cleared his throat. As he crossed his arms, his thick chest flexed. "So Lizzie's nice."

"She is."

"Not your usual type."

"And not yours, either." Which was a ridiculous thing to say but he couldn't help it.

Billy laughed. "Oh, relax yourself. I know she's off-limits. How long have you been together?"

"We're not."

"Bull."

"Fine. Let's just say…there are complications."

"Only if you want to have them."

"Please, no Dr. Phil, okay?"

Billy shrugged. "Just haven't seen you look at a woman like that before."

Don't ask. Don't ask. Don't be an idiot and— "How do I look at her?"

Idiot.

"Like you're actually seeing her."

"Whatever."

"Hey, I'm glad." Billy shoved a hand into his jeans pocket and took out a set of keys. "At least one of us might have a shot at getting married."

"I never said anything—"

"Touchy, touchy, touchy." Billy grinned and hit the car remote. As the Denali's lights flashed, the lock on the driver's side door made a little punching sound. "So you really do like her, huh?"

"Look, Billy, there's no—"

"You don't have to get defensive about it."

"I'm not being defensive!" As Billy laughed again, Sean cleared his throat. "I'm not."

"Oh. Really. Well, lemme remind you that as a line-backer, defense is my profession. So I'm good at spotting it."

"On the field, maybe."

Billy pointed to the ground. "And you're standing on grass as we speak."

While Billy got into the car and put the window down,

Sean cursed and stepped onto the sidewalk. "You going to be in town over the next couple of weeks?" he asked.

"I've got some away games, but other than that I'm here. You know, I'm sorry you missed today's match-up. But maybe you could come and watch me play some other time?"

"Yeah, absolutely."

"Bring Lizzie."

"We'll see." It would have to depend on whether she was around. God…he hoped she'd be around.

Billy stretched his arm out the window and the two gripped palms. There was a long moment as their eyes met.

"No looking back," Sean said. "We don't look back, remember?"

It was the credo they'd hung on to as scared children…then had reaffirmed as reckless college guys…and now lived out as best they could as adult men.

Billy nodded. "No looking back."

He put the car in gear and drove away.

As Sean watched the brake lights fade, he got pissed off that their father had been such a bastard. Billy might not have been hit as much, but he'd been ridden hard for being "stupid" because he was dyslexic and couldn't read very well.

Which was why he'd only been partially joking when he'd said Lizzie was out of his league because she was so smart.

"Your brother is very nice."

Sean turned around toward the house. Lizzie stood

in the front doorway, her body blocking the view inside, blocking the view to the stairs that went up.

Looking at her now, Sean didn't want her to know what had happened with his father. Ever. Nothing made him feel weaker or more ashamed than the past, and he wanted to be strong for her. He wanted to be a man for her.

Not a frightened little boy.

Besides, there was the relationship she'd had with his father. Though Sean couldn't understand it, it was clear she'd been close to the man and there was no reason to spoil her memories of him with stuff that didn't affect her.

Sean walked up onto the porch and wrapped his arms around her. As she embraced him back, he closed his eyes so he couldn't see the stairs.

"Did I tell you how beautiful you look tonight?" he said into her hair.

She chuckled a little. "This jeans and T-shirt combo isn't exactly Miss America–worthy."

He held on even harder. "The hell they aren't. To me, whatever you have on is a ball gown."

She stiffened, but then eased back into him. "You scare me when you say things like that."

"Why?"

"I'm afraid I'll start believing them."

He pulled back and looked her in the eye. "Believe them, Lizzie. Trust me and believe them."

Chapter Fourteen

The following Thursday, Lizzie raced for the phone in the living room, leaving a pot of water with a fistful of linguine in it boiling on the stove.

"Hello?"

"Hi." Sean's voice was warm over the line.

She smiled so wide her cheeks stretched. "Hi."

"How was your day?"

"Better now."

He laughed. "Funny, I feel the same way."

Over the past week, he'd surprised the hell out of her. He called her every day at least once, sometimes more often. And when she was moonlighting, no matter what time it was when she got home, the phone would ring as if he'd set his alarm to her schedule just so he could check she was safe and sound.

"Are you in a car?" she asked. "I hear a whirring noise in the background."

"Yeah, I'm on the road again."

"I don't know how you do everything you do." Boy, from what she'd learned, he earned every penny of the money he got for putting those billion-dollar deals together. He worked around the clock and there were very few times when there were no arguing voices in the background as they talked.

Yet, even though he was busy, somehow she was always his sole focus when he called. There had been numerous occasions when people had tried to interrupt and he'd put them off curtly. He even lingered over goodbyes as if he didn't want her to go. Every time.

"You sound tired," he said.

She headed back for the stove. "Just not as many daytime jobs in downtown as I'd hoped."

"Your car come back today?"

"Yes, thank heavens." She stirred the pasta with a fork. She was glad to have a set of wheels again, but cutting the check for all that work had pained her…and so was what she was about to ask him. The thing was, however, it was the end of the month and although money wasn't quite a problem, it was going to be in a little while. "Ah…Sean?"

"Mmm?"

"I hate to bring this up, but remember when you said I could live here rent free until you sold the—"

"Absolutely. Don't you dare write that check."

"Thank you…really, thank you. I hate to impose, but things are going to get tight for me."

"I'd offer you a loan, but I have a feeling you'd turn me down."

"Of course I would! But I do appreciate the break on the rent, even though I wish I didn't need it." She cradled the phone between her ear and her shoulder, picked up the pot and headed for the strainer in the sink. As she poured, a waft of steam shot up and she leaned back. "Whoa, hot."

"What is?"

"Spaghetti water." She put the pot back on the stove and jogged the strainer, making the linguine bounce. "So do you have another busy night planned?"

His voice deepened. "Oh, yeah. Very busy."

"I think you work too hard."

"Some kinds of work are a real pleasure."

"You love what you do, don't you?"

"I love what I'm going to be doing tonight." The whirring noise in the background got cut off. Then there were some dinging sounds followed by a dull *thunch*.

She poured the pasta back into the pot. "Mergers and acquisitions must really interest you."

"Mergers especially."

"What are you working on now or is it a secret—" The sound of a knock on her door brought her head around and her heart to her throat. "Sean?"

"Yes?"

She started to laugh and ran out to the living room. As she threw open the door, they both hung up their phones.

"What are you doing h—" She didn't get a chance to finish the sentence.

Sean dropped a duffel bag and dragged her against him, picking her up as he kicked the door shut. His mouth came down on hers and his hands gripped her hips as he carried her across the room.

She held on to his shoulders, so lost in the kiss she barely noticed that he was laying her on the couch and undoing the buttons down the front of her shirt…and working on the waistband of her jeans.

"I've missed my Lizzie," he growled as he peeled back one side of her bra. "Mmm…"

He closed his mouth on her nipple while he stripped off her Levi's and her underwear. Then he moved down her body, his lips going to the inside of her thigh and working their way to the very core of her.

He gave her shimmering pleasure, and when she came back into herself, she opened her eyes slowly. Sean was standing above her sprawled, satiated body, ripping off his tie and doing away with his button-down shirt. His eyes burned as he took hold of his fine leather belt and worked the buckle—then his deft fingers went to his fly and there was the sound of a zipper being dragged down.

His trousers hit the floor and she saw his arousal pushing at the thin cotton of his boxers. But then they were gone, too, his naked power revealed. She sat up, drawn by the sight of him, and encircled him with her hand.

"*Lizzie,*" he moaned, his head falling back.

She worshipped him until he made her stop by pulling her head back with a shudder. As he went for the pocket of his suit, his breathing was harsh and sweat gleamed on his muscular chest. He covered himself and got on top of her.

"I need to apologize in advance," he said with a rasp as he slipped inside.

After they both groaned, she mumbled, "For what?"

"I'm not going to last long."

And he didn't. But neither did she.

The next morning, Sean got up early and made Lizzie breakfast. He figured it was the least he could do considering the double shift she was going to pull today at the BMC emergency department.

As he fired up her coffee and got out a bowl and a spoon for her cereal, he listened to her moving around her bedroom…and realized this was probably why people got married.

Man, he loved this quiet morning peacefulness. Loved the idea he was helping her start her day. Loved the fact that when her work was done, she was going to come back and walk through the door and tell him how she'd spent the hours they'd been apart.

Domestic bliss indeed.

He put the milk carton next to the bowl and brought the box of corn flakes over from the cupboard. Not exactly eggs Benedict with hollandaise, but considering the time constraint and the fact that he only knew how to do hash-slinger stuff, she was more likely to enjoy the cereal.

"Chow's on," he called out.

She came right away and he poured the milk for her until she said when. Then he watched her eat. She was dressed in scrubs and not wearing makeup and her hair was all soft and blond and a little flyaway from the dryer.

To him she was the last word in female.

"So you're starting to pack today?" she said as she sipped her coffee.

"Yup." He leaned back with his own mug and studied the way the sunlight slanting through the kitchen window hit her cheeks and lips. He wished he had a photograph of her just as she was now, but he was going to have to rely on his memory.

"I'll help you tomorrow," she said.

"Thanks, but if you're home, I'd rather be doing other things with you." As she blushed, he tilted his head down and looked at her from under his brows. They hadn't slept much during the night because he'd been all over her. After having spent a mere five days away, he'd been insatiable. "Have I mentioned that I can't wait for you to get back tonight?" He reached out and brushed her cheek with his fingertips. "I want a repeat of how we spent last evening."

She turned even redder and kissed his palm. "Sean…"

He smiled. "I love it when you blush."

Her expression grew wry. "I do it often enough around you."

"I know."

As a soft chiming sound came from a clock, she pulled back. "Oh, darn…the time. I'm late."

When she took hold of her bowl, he said, "Don't bother cleaning up, I'll take care of it."

"You're so good to me."

"I want to be even better."

They headed for the living room together and he loved the soft, secret smile on her face—because he knew he was the cause of it.

The expression was lost as she went over to her purse and took out her wallet. Thumbing through the thing, she cursed softly.

"Not enough cash?" he said.

"I'll be okay—"

"Here." He picked up his suit jacket, pulled out his money clip and peeled off a hundred-dollar bill. "Take this."

She glanced over, eyes widening. "Oh, no…that's okay—"

"You're late, right? So it would be hard to stop at a cash machine."

"Well, yes, but at work they have—"

He pressed the crisp Benjamin Franklin into her hand and wrapped her fingers around it, finding an unfamiliar but vivid satisfaction in giving money to a woman. He just loved the idea he was helping her, providing for her. "Take it."

"Thanks, I'll pay you—"

He silenced her with a kiss. Then couldn't resist slipping his tongue between her lips. When he pulled back, he murmured, "Have I mentioned how I can't wait until you come home?"

"Yes. And I'll second that."

He walked her out into the foyer and ushered her to the front door, but hung back from the great outdoors because he only had boxers on. As she got into the old Toyota, he hated the thing she was driving. He wanted to buy her a new ride with state-of-the-art air bags and a steel crash cage and every amenity available to make her comfortable and safe.

With a wave, she pulled away from the curb and headed off. In her wake, he had to laugh at himself. Before meeting her, he'd refused to give women a dime. Now? He wanted to shower his money all over Lizzie Bond.

Not that she'd let him.

Fine. He was just going to drag his feet on the sale of the house, then. The longer he put it off, the more time Lizzie could be rent free and the less stressed she'd be as she looked for a job.

And maybe he could start working on her about the car thing.

Sean whistled as he went back in her apartment, cleaned up breakfast and started a fresh pot of coffee. He took a steaming mug upstairs with him, and as he opened the door to his father's place, he braced himself for the usual gut crank.

He was glad he hadn't eaten breakfast when it hit.

After casing the joint, he decided to start in the kitchen. It was the room with the fewest memories.

It didn't take long to develop a core competency getting those U-Haul boxes taped into shape. He filled them with dishes and glasses and cheap silverware, all of which would go to the church. He also started a trash pile. A lot of the cooking utensils were rusted from lack of use and he realized, as he threw out wire whisks and paring knives and measuring spoons, that what he was pitching had most likely last been touched by his mother.

Yeah, Eddie never had been much of a cook. Sean and his brothers had pretty much lived on peanut-butter-and-jelly sandwiches. Well, those and Mrs. O'Neal's handouts.

Sean had been in full clean-out mode for about an hour when he found a half-empty, dust-covered bottle of booze way in the back of a cupboard.

Ah, yes. The demon.

As he poured the cheap vodka out and watched the stuff funnel down the scratched porcelain sink, he wondered what quitting had been like for his father. As well as the why and the when of it.

It would have been hard, that was for sure. Alcohol and his father had been inseparable, the one relationship Eddie had valued, the one thing the man had connected with. Sean could even remember being jealous of the Popov. When Eddie wasn't loaded, he might actually talk to you.

At the very least, he didn't come after you.

A little later, Sean found another bottle in the broom closet. Again, dust-covered. This time when he emptied the booze, he didn't think of anything at all.

It took him the better part of the morning to finish up the kitchen and then he started in on the living room. As he worked, the number of stacked, marked boxes grew and he went through miles of packing tape.

He broke for eats around noon and then forced himself to hit the bedrooms. As he couldn't bear to go into his father's or Mac's, he whipped through his and Billy's then took care of the bathrooms. When he was through with them, it was only seven o'clock. Lizzie wasn't going to be home for another five hours and there was no reason to stop working.

Except all that was left were the two places he didn't want to go.

As he paused outside the door to Mac's room, he wished like hell his older brother would check in. He supposed there was always the option of trying to track Mac down through military channels, but he knew his brother wouldn't appreciate getting red flagged even if it was for a good reason. Besides, given what the guy did, it might not even be possible to find him through regular army contacts.

Sean went inside and worked fast. He needed only four boxes for Mac's stuff and then he was left with nothing but his father's domain.

Gearing up, he headed down the hall with an armful of cardboard and a taping wheel. Inside his dad's room, he flipped on the overhead light and looked around. Pretty much standard-issue, lower-middle-class stuff. The bed was made, but the blankets were old and the pillows thin. On the side table, there was a fake wood alarm clock, a lamp with a yellowed shade and a little thicket of pill bottles.

Sean went over and checked out the labels. He recognized the ones for high blood pressure and cholesterol, but the others didn't mean anything to him. Whatever. They obviously hadn't worked all that well.

He taped up a box to use as a trash bin and tossed the orange vials then emptied the drawer underneath of a bunch of old racing forms.

He was about to start stripping the bed when he saw the slippers on the floor.

The pair were right out of the L.L. Bean catalog,

made of tan leather and lined in sheep's wool. They were old and worn, peeling up off the carpet at the toes. The two were lined up right together, facing out as if his father had kicked them off as he'd gotten into the bed for what had turned out to be the last time.

God… Same kind Eddie O'Banyon had worn twenty years ago. Conceivably the very pair.

Sean picked one up. Inside, as if the soles were made of sand, there was a precise impression of his father's foot registered in relief. The man had clearly spent hours wearing them, shuffling around this apartment, crossing from room to room…until suddenly there were no more trips to be made and the slippers would never be worn again.

Thoroughly creeped out, Sean pushed them under the bed so he didn't have to see them, then took off the sheets and threw them out.

The closet was next. After opening the doors, he stared at what hung from the wooden dowel. It was the same stuff his father had always worn. Low-price button-downs—cotton for spring and summer, flannel for fall and winter—and khakis. Off to one side, there was an old work shirt from the phone company with a patch that read Eddie O'Banyon as well as a suit with a fine layer of dust on the shoulders. Probably the last time that had been worn had been at Sean's mother's funeral.

Looking at the clothes, thinking about the slippers, Sean could picture his father so clearly, it was as if the man's ghost had wandered into the room, all simmering and pissed off at being called from the grave.

To get rid of the Stephen Kings, Sean put his hand into the closet and grabbed the first thing he hit. Going on autopilot, he stripped the hangers bare then picked up the shoes from the floor and cleaned off the top shelf. He hit the dresser after that, whipping through the drawers, throwing out the underwear and socks, putting the sweaters into a box.

Final salvo in the room was the rolltop desk in the corner.

The thing was a rank, ugly, worn piece of crap that had nothing but function to offer the world. Battened down tight, with the top in place, it gave off the illusion of having something precious inside.

But only out of desperation.

As Sean slid up the cover, papers spilled out as if he'd opened some kind of wound and the POS was bleeding white.

What a mess.

Copping a seat in the hard-backed chair, he pulled over the box he was using as a waste bin and started sifting through Medicare notices and doctors' bills and insurance-company correspondence and bank statements. Most of the envelopes were unopened and he felt as if he were on an archaeological dig. The farther he went back, the older things got.

After having turfed the balance of it into some loose organizational piles, he was able to get to the shallow drawers in the back of the desk. He found nothing much important in them, just a couple of old Ticonderoga pencils, some paper clips, a thicket of rubber bands, a bottle of Elmer's glue that had turned into a solid. Everything smelled like the musky wood of the desk and the dry, dusty scent of time's passing.

He moved on to the big drawers underneath…and wasn't prepared for what he found.

He was going through what was just crap, mindlessly pitching copies of *Motor Trend* from the eighties into the trash box, when he ran into the photograph.

He sat up slowly, holding the thing with care.

Black-and-white. Three by five. Torn at the corner.

He and Billy and Mac were all under the age of twelve and standing at rigid attention in ill-fitting suits. They were smiling awkwardly, the pained expressions worn with the same graceless forbearance as their Sunday clothes.

His mother had taken the picture and her handwriting, her beautiful cursive handwriting, was on the back: the date, the place and his and his brothers' names.

Staring at the old ink, it dawned on him that in all the packing he'd done he hadn't found any photographs of her. In fact, there was nothing of hers in the apartment at all. Sure, his father hadn't been sentimental in the slightest, but wouldn't something have survived?

He turned the picture back over and tried to remember what his mother had looked like on the other side of the camera.

When he couldn't call an image to mind, he thought of Lizzie.

He wanted pictures of her. Lots of them. He wanted one at his penthouse by his bed. And one on his desk at his office. And one in his briefcase. And one stored digitally in his BlackBerry.

As if having all that would ensure she didn't disappear when she wasn't with him.

Sean put the shot of him and his brothers facedown on the top of the desk and vowed to go out and buy a camera. Like, tomorrow.

The piles of envelopes got his attention and he figured it was time to find out what kind of mess his father's estate was in. God, he hoped the man's will was in this morass somewhere, but chances were good Eddie had died intestate.

Sean started with the bank statements and got no further.

The first one he went through was from June and there were a number of checks…most of which were written to Lizzie Bond.

In her own hand.

Sean's skin shrank around his skeleton, just tightened up on his body as if he'd been put under a heat lamp and was drying out. As his breath froze in his lungs, he let the hand holding the pale green slips of paper fall to his thigh.

When he could stand it, he looked at the checks again. His father's signature was on the bottom of each one, a messy scrawl that just about screamed feeble and old and coercible.

Except maybe she'd just been writing them out at his request.

Sean quickly ripped open the other statement envelopes. Checks she'd filled out went all the way back for a year and the amounts varied from a hundred to five hundred dollars. There were four that were over a thousand.

When he was finished adding it all up, the total amount was well into the tens of thousands.

With a curse, he tossed a handful of checks onto the desk. As they scattered all around, he reached over to keep them from hitting the floor and caught sight of an envelope postmarked six weeks ago. In the left-hand corner, there was the return address of a local law firm.

As he slipped his finger under the flap, he got a paper cut that bled and he sucked off the sting while unfolding what turned out to be his father's last will and testament.

That left everything to one Miss Elizabeth Bond.

Well…well…well.

What do you know.

Turned out he and his father had something in common after all. Because like Eddie, Sean had been suckered into supporting Lizzie, too.

Man, she was smooth. He hadn't seen this coming.

Sean refolded the will and put it back in the envelope. Rage tickled the edge of his consciousness, making his head buzz, but he wasn't mad at her. He was mad at himself.

He'd been taken for a fool by a woman again and it was his own damned fault.

Chapter Fifteen

Even though it had been a tragically busy night in the emergency department, Lizzie was smiling as she got out of her car and skipped up the front steps to the duplex's porch. When she opened the door, she heard sounds from upstairs so she jogged upward.

One look at Mr. O'Banyon's living room and she stopped dead.

Stacks of U-Haul boxes were as high as her shoulders, each marked with the name of the local Catholic church. The rug that had been under the couch was rolled up and taped. The TV was unplugged and by the door. The few pictures that had hung on the walls were down and so too were the faded lace curtains.

"Good Lord, Sean," she called out. "You've worked yourself to the bone."

As she heard him coming from the back, she smiled.

Until he walked in and she saw his face.

The man who had sent her off this morning with a lingering kiss was gone. The man who had poured her cereal and watched her eat and cleaned up her dishes was nowhere to be seen. The lover she had taken into her body and slept beside had been replaced by a hard, cynical stranger.

"Well, I'd better get packing," he said in a clipped tone. "I've got to get out of your way."

"Excuse me?"

He held out a sheath of documents. "Congratulations, your charm worked. Not twice, mind you. But at least you got the house from him plus whatever cash is left in his accounts."

As his words spun around in her brain, Lizzie felt as if she were midway through a car accident. Everything slowed down and she braced herself for imminent impact. What she didn't know was just how bad the injuries were going to be.

"What are you talking about?"

He pushed the papers at her. "Surely you've got your own copy of this?"

Putting her purse down on a box, she took what was in his hand. After she finished reading the will, she looked up in disbelief.

"I didn't ask him to do this. I don't want the house. Or the money."

"Oh, really." The smile that came at her was horrible. Just a baring of teeth. "You know, I have to give you credit. I mean, you had me, you really did."

"Sean, I didn't—"

"I'm sure you're going to get a good price for this place. And soon, too. I'm almost finished here so you can put it on the market right away. Or keep it. Either way, you won't have to worry about rent for a while and not just because some sap is letting you live here for free."

"Why in the world do you think I'd—"

"I saw the checks."

"What?"

"The ones you wrote to yourself and made him sign."

Lizzie was momentarily speechless. But then she had plenty of things to say. "I *beg* your pardon. First of all, your father's hands shook from the meds he was on and it was hard for him to write. Secondly, those checks were to me to reimburse what *I* spent on *him*. He was all but housebound because of his heart and the only way I could get him to let me do his errands was if he paid me up front. And we *still* fought about it all the time. He hated accepting help."

"A plausible denial, but you have no way of proving to me where any of this cash went, do you? Unless you have receipts from the past year, which somehow I doubt you're going to be able to produce. Bottom line? There's a lot more gone from here than can be accounted for through food expenses and miscellaneous purchases. And though I'm sure you're one hell of a cleaning lady, I don't think a good dusting is that expensive."

Lizzie shook her head and thought of all the prescriptions she'd filled and doctor's office co-pays she'd covered and cardiac rehab visits she'd shelled out for. And that was just the tip of the iceberg for what treating his heart had required.

But she wasn't going to justify herself. Sean wouldn't believe anything she told him and she was so angry at him she was likely to fly off the handle.

"You don't trust me at all, do you?" she said.

"Give me one reason, in the face of all this, that I should."

"Wow. Yeah…that's all I've got right now. Just…wow." She picked up her purse and put the will on a box. "You can keep the house, Sean. I wouldn't take it if you paid me to."

"Uh-huh, right. A convenient show, but legally it's already yours."

"I never asked him for this. And I can't believe you find it so easy to doubt me. But you know what? I'd rather know about your lack of faith sooner rather than later." She turned to the door and stared at him over her shoulder. "I've been telling myself you're just slow to trust, but I don't think that's actually true. I think you're broken, Sean…on the inside. So this showdown between us was inevitable, and although it hurts like hell, I'm glad it's out of the way. I'll put your things out in the foyer in a couple of minutes. Don't knock on my door again. Ever."

Chapter Sixteen

Sean spent the night at the Four Seasons and returned to the duplex to let the church folks in the following morning. Lizzie was working another double shift so she wasn't around. Which was good.

His father's place was empty by 11:00 a.m. and he was on his plane going back to Manhattan not long thereafter.

During the flight, he got no work done. Made no phone calls. Ate nothing, drank nothing. He sat alone in the luxurious cabin and tried to convince his brain to shut up. It was a debate he lost. The refrain that he'd been taken as a fool again just kept hammering at him, making him feel stupid and as if he shouldn't ever trust his instincts. God, he'd been so careful. For years. To be taken unawares again challenged his faith in himself.

And the worst of it all? There was a little voice in his head that doubted what he'd seen with his own eyes…. That wanted to believe Lizzie Bond wasn't capable of that kind of cunning… That craved to find out a different truth.

Anytime that whisper got too loud, though, he just reminded himself about all those checks and that will. Also recalled that desperation was no one's friend…and he'd very certainly been desperate for that woman.

God, he was an *idiot*.

As the plane circled Teterboro Airport before landing, his phone went off in his pocket. He frowned at the caller ID on the BlackBerry. Untraceable.

"Hello?"

"Sean O'Banyon?" came a male voice.

"Yeah."

"This is in regard to your brother, Sergeant Major Mark David O'Banyon."

Sean's blood ran cold until it was a solid in his veins. "Yes?"

"I understand you've left a number of messages for him. He's on special assignment right now and will not be able to respond to them for a period of time. This is a courtesy call."

Sean got dizzy from relief. Nearly saw stars. "Any idea when I'll hear from him? There's been a death in the family and I'd prefer not to tell him over the phone."

"I can't answer that in any official manner. But you might think in terms of months, not days. I can, however, try and get a message to him. If this is vital."

"Our father's dead."

There was a pause. "You have my condolences and

I will make sure that he gets the news. Is there anything else?"

God, there were so many other things he wanted to tell Mac, but not through an intermediary. "No. I'll wait to hear from him, but thanks for this."

"He will get the word. You can trust the army."

"I do. Thanks again."

Sean hung up and the plane descended. As the wheels squeaked on the tarmac, he remembered that tonight was the Hall Foundation Gala and he was going as Elena's social shield.

Damn shame he was feeling so transparent.

On Sunday, Lizzie went to the local market and bought the *Boston Globe* for its classifieds section and the *New York Times* for the crossword puzzle. Back at home, she sat on her couch, turned on National Public Radio for company and got out a red pen to circle jobs and apartments.

As she went through the rental section, and looked at addresses and monthly costs, she was nothing but an ache with arms and legs. Her whole body hurt, but the worst of it was in her chest. And she couldn't get her mind to focus. Eventually, she ended up doodling until her pen ate a hole in the newspaper and ink bled through onto her thigh.

She licked her forefinger and rubbed the red mark away.

She was so angry at Sean. Insulted. Hurt. Offended.

Now there was a crossword-puzzle theme. All the emotions you felt when you were grossly misjudged by someone. Probably wouldn't fly though. PISSED OFF was not likely to show up in the *Times* as a clue. And neither was WEEPY AS HELL.

As she started in on another corner with the doodling, part of her wanted to call Sean and yell at him. Part of her wanted to prove she wasn't who he thought she was. And part of her just wanted to crawl into bed and cry.

Determined not to fall into self-pity, she reminded herself that she had three interviews lined up this week and there were a couple of apartments that might work depending on whether their bathrooms were inhabitable. So she wasn't trapped in this apartment and there were prospects for work.

God... the will.

She'd never expected Mr. O'Banyon to leave her anything. They'd never even talked about that kind of thing. And she would have told him no if they had.

Which was maybe why it hadn't come up.

The thing was, even though she was mad at Sean, and even though he had so much money it wasn't as if he needed any cash, she didn't want to take his father's legacy away from him and his brothers. That was inappropriate. And Mr. O'Banyon shouldn't have done it. His children should have come first, no matter what had broken apart the family.

She tossed the *Globe* aside and picked up the *Times*. The massive weight of Manhattan's famous paper was awkward in her hand and the thing spilled out onto the floor.

Which was how she saw Sean on the front page of

the Style section holding a superbly dressed woman in his arms.

For a moment, Lizzie considered running for the bathroom to throw up.

Even eyed the way down the hall.

Sean had said he wasn't seeing anyone else in Manhattan and she believed him. He might be a terrible judge of character, but she knew instinctively he wasn't a liar.

He just hadn't waited long at all to move on.

And what a beautiful woman he'd picked. She looked like a model. Except for her jewelry. Those rubies marked her as a queen.

Lizzie stood and went to her bedroom. Opening up the closet, she pulled out a bag and started to pack for an overnight. It had been a while since she'd been up to see her mother and now was a terrific time to get out of this apartment.

Chapter Seventeen

Six weeks later, Billy O'Banyon sat in a lawyer's office in Southie and wanted to be just about anywhere else on the planet. It wasn't that he didn't want to help Sean out with settling their father's accounts and whatnot. He just hated being around all the books and the paperwork and the kind of people who were confident with writing and reading.

The printed word and him were not friends and anytime he got into situations like this, he always felt like the stupid idiot his father had told him he was.

But whatever. He was going to be out of here and back in the gym within the hour. As their father's will was uncontested and going through probate quickly enough, this wasn't going to be a long meeting. All he had to do was deliver some unpaid bills to the lawyer who was the estate's executor and discuss how the deed transfer and house vacating were going to go.

Actually, being here was his own fault. He could easily have mailed the stuff or dropped it off, but he was a man with a mission. He wanted to run into Lizzie Bond and this was the only acceptable excuse he had.

Sean had been in a bad way for the past month and a half, ever since those two had broken it off. Naturally he wouldn't talk much about what had happened, so Billy wanted to see how the other side was doing. If Lizzie came in looking as if she'd been run over by a John Deere, as well, he was going to get involved. The pair had been good together and sometimes people needed a little nudge to get back on track.

Just call him a romantic. Who happened to be able to bench press five hundred pounds.

"The other party is on their way."

Billy looked up at the voice. The guy who walked into the room was dressed in a gray suit and had a lot of files in his hand. The glasses he wore were more practical than stylish, but they made him look intelligent. Then again, he probably looked that way with contacts, too.

Billy shook the hand that was offered to him and the attorney sat down. With utter nonchalance, the guy started flipping through a file, his eyes scanning text quickly.

Billy watched with envy. Man, what was that like, to easily read what was on a page? To him, words were more like jumbled patterns, abstract shapes without meaning.

The lawyer scribbled something in a margin and looked up. "So you're a football player, I guess."

Billy nodded. "Yeah, I am."

"For the Pats."

"Yeah."

"I've never been into football, but I've heard about you." The tone was vaguely censorious and Billy was used to that. It had been years since he'd grabbed headlines for being a hard-partying playboy, but people didn't forget. At least not in New England.

"I'm really all about the game now," Billy said.

"Which is, of course, why they pay you all that money." The lawyer flushed as if he'd let the words fly without thinking.

"Sorry to keep you waiting," a woman said. "Work emergency."

Billy glanced over. In the doorway, a handsome African American woman dressed in a bloodred suit was standing just outside the conference room. With her kind, smart eyes, she looked like the sort of person who could run the whole country.

Or should be running the country.

Was she Lizzie Bond's attorney?

"Not to worry," the lawyer said. "This won't take long."

The woman came forward and extended her hand to Billy. "Hi, I'm Dr. Denisha Roberts, the executive director of the Roxbury Community Health Initiative."

Billy got to his feet and leaned across the table. "Pleased to meet you."

"Do you have the power of attorney?" the lawyer asked Dr. Roberts.

"Right here." The woman took some papers out of her briefcase and sat down.

"I'm sorry," Billy cut in. "Isn't Lizzie Bond supposed to be here?"

Dr. Roberts smiled as she pushed the documents over to the lawyer. "No reason for her to be. I have to say, this is a really generous thing she's doing."

"What's she doing?"

"Giving the community center the house. It's going to be the basis of our endowment—" Dr. Roberts's eyes popped. "Wait… Are you one of his sons?"

He nodded. "Yeah, but it's okay. We don't want the house."

Which, evidently, Lizzie didn't, either. God, she was just giving the thing away?

The lawyer looked up from reviewing the power of attorney.

"This is all in order." He glanced at Billy. "Do you have the final bill from the hospital stay when he passed?"

Billy blinked. He couldn't believe Lizzie was giving an entire house away.

Dr. Roberts leaned forward and put her hand on his arm. "I want you to know that your father's going to be remembered at our health center. The endowment is going to be called the Edward O'Banyon Fund. At Lizzie's request."

Son of a bitch.

Later that afternoon, Lizzie had all but finished packing up her apartment. As she wasn't officially moving out for another three days, she left her clothes in the dresser and in the closet, but pretty much everything else was in boxes.

She couldn't wait to get out of the duplex.

Her new place was on the dark side of Beacon Hill, a stone's throw from Mass General, where she'd found a job as a floor nurse in the surgical intensive care unit.

Like the studio apartment she'd rented, her new job was going to be fine. She knew a couple of the folks she'd be working with and they were good people. Also, her supervisor had an excellent reputation and had seemed really great throughout the interview process. Of course, she'd much rather have stayed with the community center, but she hadn't lost that connection. She volunteered there on Saturday mornings.

So it had all worked out.

For the most part.

Unfortunately, no amount of positive news got her mind off Sean. Memories of him were shadows that lurked in her thoughts. She remained angry and frustrated, but there were other things she felt, too. Sadness. Loneliness.

Except she had to let it all go, let him go. There was no getting over what he'd said to her or what he'd assumed she'd done. No healing that breach of trust. Besides, he had walked away without looking back. She needed to do the same.

It was so hard, though.

When her phone started ringing, she picked it up. "Hello?"

Her mother's voice was curiously level. "Lizzie?"

"Hi, Mom." When there was just silence on the other end, she frowned. "Mom? Are you okay?"

"Yes, Lizzie-fish. It's just…the oddest thing has happened."

"What?" Oh God. "Mom? You there?"

"Someone likes my pottery."

Lizzie deflated from relief. And exhaustion. "That's great, Mom."

"They really like it."

"I can see why." Unlike a lot of her mother's "work," the pottery was gorgeous, both decorative and functional. The vases were all flowing, organic lines; the mugs wistful and quirky; the plates uneven and charming. When Lizzie had seen some of it during her overnight trip to Essex, the first thing she'd thought was that the objects were just like her mother: beautiful and fey and somehow not of this world.

"Well, the someone wants to sell them, Lizzie."

"Boy, wouldn't that be great." A little extra money was always good. "Is it the little craft store next to the grocery?"

"It's the Mason Gallery in Boston. On Newbury Street."

Lizzie's eyes popped. "What?"

"Mr. Mason was up here buying antiques with his wife and I happened to be taking a stroll with my morning coffee. He saw my mug and when I told him I made it and had others they came back to the house. He liked what I did and wants to send a truck to pick up fifty pieces."

Good…*Lord*. The Mason Gallery specialized in selling one-of-a-kind objets d'art to the high-rent crowd in Boston. Lizzie had only ever walked by the window because she knew the prices inside were way out of her league.

"What should I do, Lizzie?"

"Well, do you want to sell your work?"

"I think so." There was a slight pause and then her mother's voice grew soft, almost ashamed. "But, Lizzie, you know I'm not good with money. Will you take care of all that stuff? I mean, I am not…good with money."

Lizzie closed her eyes, knowing there was so much more in that comment. Her mother was rarely self-aware, but in this moment, she was totally present and obviously clear about her mental deficiency.

The shame was painful to hear. And so very unnecessary.

"Mom, don't worry, I'll take care of everything. I'll tell you what we have to do."

There was sigh of relief. "Thank you. Because you know what? I really like pottery. I could see myself doing this for a long while. I think I'm not just inspired, I think I'm good at it."

Lizzie blinked away the tears that pooled in her eyes. "That's wonderful, Mom. I think that's wonderful."

"You know, Lizzie…you take such good care of me. Except I was thinking last night, I kind of wish someone would take care of you. Or don't you want that?"

Lizzie had to rub her eyes. "I don't know, I'm pretty self-sufficient. I do well on my own."

Like a cheerful bird call, a dinging sound rang out in the background. "Oh, Lizzie…I must go. I have some mugs ready to come out of the kiln now. They're so pretty. Bright blue like a summer sky on the outside, white as clouds on the inside. The rims are sunshine-yellow. I'm calling it my July series."

Lizzie thought back to the morning she and Sean had walked out into the sunlight and both seen the same beauty in the day.

In a raw voice she said, "That sounds lovely, Mom. Just…lovely."

When Lizzie hung up the phone, she replayed the conversation in her head to try and keep herself from thinking of Sean.

She'd only ever heard that serious tone of voice from her mom a couple of times before. The subject had been her love for Lizzie's father—the one constant in the woman's life. So chances were good this interest in pottery was going to stick.

Lizzie put the phone back in the charger and went into her spare bedroom. She'd put the majority of boxes in here to keep them out of her way, and as she looked at her things, she counted the times she'd moved in her life. Out of home to college. Dorm changes. Nursing school. First apartment. Then this one.

She would like a home, she thought. A place to be permanent in…where the front door and the interior rooms were a constant through the seasons of the years.

But she was probably going to be a vagabond for a while yet.

As she glanced at the boxes, she thought, yeah, she and U-Haul were going to be dating for a couple more years. Vagabonds needed to take their stuff with them. And that meant boxes and bubble wrap.

With a long exhale, she went over to the closet and

figured she might as well pack up the winter clothes that were stored there.

As she opened the door, she saw something on the floor inside that brought her to a halt.

It was a tool box. A beaten-up tool box that was painted red, but so scuffed and old it was more like a dull brown. On the side, the telephone company's name was stamped in yellow block letters.

Bending down, she picked it up by the worn black handle and put it on a waist-high stack of cartons.

Mr. O'Banyon's tool box.

He'd given it to her about a month before he'd died, had insisted that she take it with her downstairs after one of their Sunday dinners. When she'd asked him why, he'd told her that he wanted it in safekeeping, that he could only trust her with what was inside. At the time, she hadn't understood why a bunch of tools were in such danger in his apartment, but he'd been agitated from a switch in his meds and a little paranoid, so she'd taken the thing.

Out of curiosity and because the sight of it made her miss her friend, Lizzie flipped free the silver clips in front and opened the lid.

Only to frown.

It was full of papers, not tools. Papers and…photographs.

Which kind of made sense because it wasn't the dead weight it should have been.

Lizzie reached in and took out the picture that was on top of the pile. It was a black-and-white photo of a young, dark-haired woman who was standing in front of what could only be described as a palatial mansion. She was wearing a sundress and staring out at the camera with a lovely, flirtatious smile.

Sean's mother?

Lizzie delved farther into the box and found birth certificates for Mark David, Sean Thomas and William John O'Banyon. As well as a death certificate for Anne Whitney O'Banyon. There were also faded report cards bearing Sean's name. Clippings from the *Globe* featuring Billy on the football field. A commendation from the army for Captain Mark D. O'Banyon.

Way at the bottom, there was a bunch of papers that were folded up and secured with a thin rubber band.

She had no intention of reading them. She truly didn't. In fact, she was feeling bad enough for intruding on things that were Sean's and his brothers'.

But then the old rubber band broke and the documents unfurled.

At the top of the first page she saw three words: *Child Protective Services.*

God help her, she kept reading.

When she was finished, her knees were so weak, she had to sit on the bare floor.

In his office in Manhattan, Sean swiveled his chair around so that he faced the bank of windows behind his desk. Outside, a gorgeous September day was spilling sunshine all over the skyscrapers of Wall Street.

Exhausted, tense, in a nasty-bastard mood, he decided as a public service that he would leave a little early tonight and go for a run in Central Park.

Unfortunately, the plan made him think back to the last time he'd run around outside.

That glorious afternoon with Lizzie at the Esplanade.

Putting his hand under his tie, he felt for his cross through his shirt. As he traced the outline of the crucifix, he pictured her after she'd found it in the grass, a smile on her face, the gold necklace swinging from her fingertips, the holy pendant catching the sunlight.

God, he missed her. Even though he shouldn't.

On some level, he still found it hard to believe she'd done what she had. But as a practical matter, it was difficult to repudiate what he'd seen with his own eyes.

As a finance guy, he knew that cashed checks didn't lie.

"Mr. O'Banyon?"

He swung the chair back around and looked over his paper-riddled desk. Andrew Frick and Freddie Wilcox were standing in the door to his office, the two young guys looking tired, but very pleased with themselves.

"Hey, boys, what's doing?" Sean said.

Andrew came forward and put a four-inch-thick file on the desk, all the while glowing like a kid who was turning an apple in to the teacher. "We're finished with the analysis."

Sean leafed through the documents a little. "Nice. Very nice. Must have kept you two up all night."

"It did, but it's like what you say, you can sleep when you're dead."

Sean closed the file. "Yeah. Right."

Damn... All of a sudden, he wanted to give them a

pep talk about the evils of sinking too much into your work. He wanted to warn them that long hours hardened you and relentless competition drained you and meanwhile life slipped by and you didn't even notice how alone you were.

He wished he could give them a Frisbee and tell them to hit the park and run around barefoot and get dirty and then go home and have a few beers and call up a woman they liked and hang out.

Unfortunately, he had no credibility when it came to R & R. And besides, both of the guys had the glow of the converted in their eyes. They were clearly committed to fighting their way to the top and the over-caffeinated, messianic zeal with which they looked at him suggested he was their poster boy for success.

Man, he remembered having that burn, that drive, that need to win. And he knew what it meant. Nothing was going to derail them.

"Listen, boys, get some shut-eye tonight, if you can," he said because it was the best he could do.

"As long as you don't need anything else from us?"

"No, Andrew, this is what I wanted. I'll check through it tonight, but I have a feeling it's going to be a spotless numbers crunch. Glad you guys are on my team."

The two positively walked on air as they left.

In their wake, Sean felt as old as a stone and just about as lively.

When his BlackBerry went off, he took it out and answered before checking caller ID. He knew who it was going to be. Had been waiting for the call all afternoon.

"What happened at the lawyer's, Billy? Did you see her?"

Except the caller on the other end wasn't his younger brother. "Sean?"

"Mac? Is that you?"

"Yeah." His older brother's voice was thin and raspy, no doubt because he was calling from the other side of the flipping planet. "It's me."

God... What to say? "You heard about Dad? You got my message?"

"You bury him yet?"

"Ashes have been interred."

"Next to Mom?"

"Yeah." There was a pause and the silence made Sean twitchy. Mac was not a big talker under the best of circumstances and it had been a long time since they'd had any contact. But Sean felt as if he had to milk the precious seconds for all they were worth. "So, you sound really far away."

"You okay with him being gone?"

Sean swiveled his chair around so he could see the sky again. He wondered what part of the heavens his brother was under. "Yeah. Fine. Relieved, maybe."

"What about Billy?"

"Same." Sean cleared his throat. Knew he wasn't going to get anything, but asked anyway, "And you?"

"I'm coming home."

Sean sat forward in a rush. "You are?"

"Yeah."

"When?"

"Month or so."

"Are you out?"

"Think I could stay with Billy? In Boston?"

Nicely dodged, that discharge question. "Of course. You want me to tell him?"

"Yeah. When I get closer to my release date, I'll let him know."

"Release date? So you're really getting out?"

"Take care, Sean. Same to Billy. I'll be in touch."

The call ended. And Mac was gone like a ghost.

But at least he was coming home. God, how long had it been since Mac had been to the States for any period of time? Years.

Idly, Sean wondered what his brother looked like now. He'd be forty.

The BlackBerry went off again and this time Sean checked who it was before answering. Billy. Finally.

"Mac just called," he said instead of *hello*.

There was a sharp inhale. "He did?"

"Yeah, he's coming stateside and wants to stay with you in Boston for a little while."

"Whoa. I mean, of course he can bunk at my house here. Thing's big enough for an army." Billy paused, then asked, "What did he sound like?"

"The same. Distant. No idea where he was. Call lasted all of about half a minute."

"At least he's coming home."

"That's what I was thinking." After a brief pause, Sean switched the subject. "So did you see her?"

"No."

"What?" Sean frowned. "Lizzie didn't show?"

"Didn't have to because she's not the one taking

over the house. She gave it to the Roxbury Community Health Initiative. The director came with a power of attorney. Said they're going to use the sale of it to start the center's endowment. And get this, Lizzie asked that the fund be named after Dad."

Sean felt all the blood drain out of his head. A horrible, surreal feeling of doom cloaked him until he was mostly blind and mostly deaf and almost dead in his chair.

Gold diggers most certainly did not give away assets like that.

"I gotta go, Billy. Call you later."

Chapter Eighteen

As night eased over South Boston, a blanket of black heat came in and settled down for the evening.

Lizzie sat in the armchair, right next to the air conditioner, holding her phone in her hands. She tried to dial Sean's number again. And failed.

She just couldn't complete the call to him. One reason was the obvious issue of the way things had been left between them. The other was far more complex.

The tool box had to be returned and it wasn't the kind of thing she felt comfortable just leaving outside the apartment upstairs. As she'd long forgotten how to reach Billy, that left Sean. But what to say?

She collapsed back into the chair and her eyes slid

over to the tool box. For the millionth time, she thought about the papers she'd read.

Mr. O'Banyon, her old friend, was not who she'd thought he was.

Or maybe he'd transformed himself through the years into someone else completely. She couldn't imagine the man she'd known doing what those papers had stated, except it was clear he had.

Things to atone for indeed.

And Sean… Poor Sean. Her heart ached for the little boy he'd been. Ached also for Billy. And for the brother she hadn't met.

The papers had been a report of a domestic abuse complaint and its follow-up. Evidently, the oldest boy, Mac, had missed several days of school. When he'd finally shown up again, he'd gone to gym class, taken off his shirt and one of the teachers had seen the faded marks on his body. Which had triggered the complaint and investigation.

The boys had been taken from the home for two months then returned. All three of them had maintained Mac's contusions had come from street fighting, not their father. Which was, of course, not unusual. Often children protected their parents out of love or fear of retribution or any one of a number of rationales.

Lizzie was willing to bet things hadn't improved when they'd come home. The two months of anger-management counseling Mr. O'Banyon had received back in 1979 likely hadn't turned things around. Especially if he'd continued to drink. Which she was willing to bet he had.

Goddamn it, she would never get answers out of him, would she? She would never be able to confront him. She would never know how long or why or whether what he'd done had eaten him alive as she hoped it had.

Mr. O'Banyon was gone. Dead.

Though the past lived on, didn't it?

As a nurse, she'd seen the tragedies of domestic abuse and she'd talked to some social workers about the wide-ranging effects it had on its victims. One corollary for survivors, which tended to persist through adulthood, was trust issues in relationships. Particularly intimate ones.

So she found it difficult to stay angry with Sean for the conclusions he'd drawn about her character. She didn't appreciate his misconceptions, but at least now she could understand how he'd be predisposed to making them. Especially given the fact that someone had likely once used him for money.

Okay, enough with the thinking. Time to call him.

She started to dial just as she heard a car pull up in front of the house.

On some sixth sense, she leaned forward and looked out the window. Through the blinds, she saw Sean get out of a rental car.

Their eyes met. In the glow of a streetlight, she saw he was wearing another one of his suits and that this time his tie was a brilliant blue. He looked just as she remembered him: handsome, powerful, strong.

A car passed between them. Then with his typical masculine grace, he lifted a hand.

When she raised her palm in response, he started for the house. With long strides, he crossed the street and she heard his footsteps on the front porch.

She opened her door just as he came into the duplex. The cologne she remembered so clearly wafted in, going deep into her nose.

"Hi," he said.

"Hi." All she could think about as she stared at him was what she'd read in that report. She wanted to put her arms around him, hold him tight, ease him. "I was just about to call you."

His brows shot up. "Really?"

"I, ah, found something that belonged to your father." She motioned him in. When he walked into the living room, she shut the door. "It's right here."

She lifted up the tool box and his eyes latched onto the thing.

"God, I can remember him taking that to work all the time." Sean reached out and took it from her. "Guess it's one more donation to the church."

"You need to look inside before you give it away."

Sean's eyes narrowed. Then he put the thing on her couch and opened the lid. As he peered in, his breath left his lips on a long exhale. He picked up the photograph of his mother with reverence.

"So he kept one picture after all," Sean said softly. "I'd wondered. I didn't find any while I was cleaning up."

Lizzie crossed her arms over her chest and covered her mouth with her hand. She hated the strain in his voice, despised its cause.

He rifled through the contents, looking at the birth

certificates and then…the Child Protective Services report.

After he scanned the document, he folded the papers back up. "You read this, didn't you?"

"It was wrong of me, but yes, I did." She sighed. "I'm so sorry, Sean. I had no idea. None. And from what I knew of your father, I wouldn't have guessed him capable of it." When he stayed silent, she said, "I'm very sorry I intruded on your privacy. I'll say nothing, of course. To anyone."

Sean went over to the windows. Against the backdrop of the blinds, his profile was rigid and so were his shoulders.

Lizzie wanted to jump out of her skin as he stood there for the longest time. Was he mad at her? Was he back in the past? What should she do?

His voice drifted over to her. "You know, in retrospect, I'm surprised they let us go back." He tapped the papers against his palm. "Although I guess they really bought the 'we're just rough-and-tumble boys and that's why we have bruises' routine. I wish now that we hadn't been so persuasive."

"Was it the drinking?" she asked quietly. "Your father mentioned to me once he'd struggled with it."

"Yeah, he did what he did only when he was drunk. And hell, even though he got into the sauce every night, it wasn't all the time that he came after us. It was just…you didn't know when it was going to happen so it felt like every day even if there were months of relative quiet." His hazel eyes shifted over to her. "It's okay, though. We're fine now. Everything is fine."

"It's okay if you're not."

"No, it isn't."

Feeling as if she were intruding, but unable to stop because of her concern for him, she said, "Sean, have you ever talked to someone about what happened?"

He frowned. "Talked?"

"Like to a therapist."

"God, no. No need to. Like I said, we're fine." He stared at her. "I wish you didn't know."

"Sean…there's no shame in it. It wasn't your fault."

He looked away. And started to blink a lot.

"You didn't do anything wrong, Sean."

He swallowed with a grimace, as if he had a lump in his throat. "Yeah, I know."

"Do you?"

He swept a quick hand over his face. "Yeah. Yeah, absolutely."

"Sean—"

His tone was hard as he interrupted her. "I really wish you didn't know. Because you were friends with my father and it would have been better for you to remember him without this. Easier."

"I'd rather have the truth. And I am angry at him. I can't *imagine* how anyone could do what he did. Damn it, I want to go back in time and take you three out of that apartment so that you got free of it. I really—" She stopped herself and forced her tone to level out. Her getting fired up was not going to help Sean. He was looking really tense, as if he were about to bolt. "I do want to tell you something, though. As I think back to some of my conversations with your father, I believe he regretted his past. And in the two years I knew him, he never touched a drop of alcohol."

"Did he say when he quit?"

"No, but I think it was a long while ago. Once, when I was cleaning up some detergent that had spilled in a cupboard, I found a stashed bottle way in the back. It was dusty."

"I found a couple of those, too."

As Sean took a deep breath and looked up at the ceiling, she saw him not as he stood before her now, all tall and powerful. She pictured him as a young boy, scared and fragile. "I'm so sorry, Sean."

"Don't say that." His voice cracked and he scrubbed his face again.

"Sean…" She started for him, but he stepped away and she let him go.

"Yeah…" He passed his palm over his eyes again and collected himself. "So, Lizzie, do you want to know why I came tonight?"

She frowned. Why *had* he shown up out of the blue? "Yes…"

"I heard from Billy. Who went to the lawyer's today. He told me that you're giving this house away to the center."

She wrapped her arms around her waist. "Oh… Well… They need the money. And as I told you, I didn't ask for that bequest."

Sean walked over to some of the boxes she'd packed and ran his hand across them. His profile was characteristically handsome, all broad lines and dark hair.

"God…Lizzie…I really wish I could undo what I

said to you. What I thought about you. What I stupidly believed you were capable of. If you'd been after my father's money you wouldn't have let this house go. So those checks… They really were for his expenses, weren't they?"

"Yes."

He cursed. "I swear I've never been wrong so many times about a woman in my whole damn life."

"It's okay."

"How can you say that?"

She took a deep breath. "I guess…because now I understand you a little more, it's easier to forgive."

Sean looked over his shoulder. Lizzie was staring at him with impossibly warm eyes, offering him only absolution and tolerance.

Damn it, he wanted her to yell at him, felt as if he deserved nothing less.

Especially because he was enough of a bastard to want to take advantage of her pity.

"You can forgive me, huh," he murmured. "I'm lucky, then. Because if I were in your shoes, I probably wouldn't be able to."

"We're different, then."

"Yeah, we are." She was a saint. He was a son of a bitch. "I'm truly sorry, Lizzie. More than you'll ever know. We were going in a great direction for a while there. You were the first woman I'd cared about in a long, long time and…hell, I blew my shot at what I've always wanted but didn't think I could have, because I have no faith."

He went back to the window and looked out to the street.

He didn't hear her come up to him, just felt a soft touch on his shoulder. As the contact was made, he whipped his head around, surprised.

"The thing about forgiveness," she said, "is that it means you let things go. You start fresh in a different place."

Sean's heart began to pound with crazy hope. But then he figured she was just talking about resolving the mess he'd created and moving on as friends. Or more likely acquaintances. Still, that was better than nothing.

"I'll take anything you're willing to give me, Lizzie. Knowing I don't deserve it."

She reached up to his face. "But you do. We all deserve good things out of life. Each one of us deserves kindness and warmth…and love."

His arms moved of their own volition and gathered her against him. He had to force himself to hold her loosely because he wanted to crush her to him.

"Thank you," he said roughly into her hair.

Sean closed his eyes and let the world recede until all he knew was the feel of her warmth and the smell of Ivory soap. His eyes stung at the thought that their paths were not going to ever cross again. The idea of leaving her on a friendly note was more tolerable than them parting as they'd been before. But it was still horrible.

She pulled back first and he let her go.

As he scrambled for some excuse to linger, she said, "I want you to go see someone, though."

He blinked. "I'm sorry?"

"If we're going to be together, I need you in therapy. I'm willing to cut you all kinds of emotional slack, but I want you working on what happened, okay? Because the truth is, you're not fine. You've got things you need to talk about that require professional help. And unless you get it, we're just going to end up here again, over something else."

All he could do was stare at her. First, because he wasn't sure he'd heard her right. And then because he figured he had and they might still have something…and how many times in life did a miracle fall in your lap?

"Lizzie, I'm sorry…. Can you be a little clearer? My hearing's fine, but my brain's shorted out."

She laughed a little. "I want to be with you still. If it's something you want."

"Oh…God. Oh, Lizzie…I don't deserve this—"

She cut him off. "I'll be honest with you. If it weren't for your past, I probably wouldn't give things another shot. But because I know what you've been through, I guess I feel as though the not-trusting thing is understandable. I mean, that's hard for you, right? Trusting people."

He found himself nodding. "Yeah… Yeah, it really is."

"Makes sense. If you grew up in a situation where things were out of control and scary, where you never felt safe, of course that would be hard. But relationships require trust. So if we're going to be in one, you need to talk to someone—"

Sean dragged her against him and held her so hard they were one body not two.

He dropped his head to her neck and said, "I'll see someone. I swear to you. I'll do anything to have you in my life. I'm that desperate. I'm that needy for you."

He started kissing her and then she was kissing him back and then they were on the couch in a blaze of passion. Clothes flew and someone had to run down to the bedroom for some protection and they ended up on the floor, but it was utterly glorious.

When the rush was spent and they were in the afterglow, Lizzie glanced over at the tool box.

"Sean...how would you feel about naming the endowment after your mother? I think I'd rather have her name on it."

Sean's chest ached at her thoughtfulness, her strength, her kindness.

"I think...I think that would be perfect." He tucked a piece of hair behind her ear. "I think that would be perfect...just like you."

Epilogue

Two months later...

Standing in the bathroom of her studio on Beacon Hill, Lizzie looked at herself in a full-length mirror and didn't recognize who was staring back at her. The woman in the reflection was wearing a black gown and her hair was curled and her makeup was…well, hell, the makeup was fabulous—thanks to help from one of the ladies at the Chanel counter at Macy's.

"You look beautiful," Sean said from behind her.

She glanced at him in the glass. He was dressed in a tuxedo and a crisp white shirt and a black bow tie.

"So do you," she said, smiling.

He slipped his arms around her waist and pulled

her back against his chest. "But I think there's something missing."

She gathered up some of the gown's skirting then let the chiffon run through her fingers. "Are you kidding me? This dress is perfect. Well, maybe it's a little long, but I like the train effect."

Boy, she couldn't believe she was in something like this, a Vera Wang dress. Or that she was going to a gala fund-raiser…for the Roxbury Community Health Initiative. It was going to be an amazing night. The governor, Jack Walker, was going to speak and the money raised would go to the Anne W. O'Banyon endowment for the center.

Sean came around in front of her. "So you think the skirt's too long?"

He eased down on one knee and tugged lightly at the dress. As he did, he had a little half smile on his face, a secret grin that she'd learned he only gave to her.

Over the past two months, they'd seen each other every weekend, either because he flew up or she flew down. They talked on the phone constantly, usually way into the night, and it was safe to say that things were way better than good.

He'd kept his promise and started to see a therapist, even though she knew bringing up the past was hard on him. When he'd call her afterward and talk to her about the sessions, she could hear the emotion in his voice, but he'd made a commitment and he didn't stop going. No matter how difficult it was.

Because her man was like that. Strong.

"I think the length is perfect," he said.

"Still, maybe being in heels is better." She glanced over her shoulder at a shoe box that was next to the sink. Then turned back. "Could you pass me—"

Lizzie's mouth dropped open and her heart stopped beating.

Sean had taken a small leather box out of somewhere and was holding it up to her with the lid closed.

"What is that?" she whispered.

"Like I said, I thought you were missing something." His eyes were warm and grave as he opened the thing.

A diamond the size of a thumb glinted out of a black velvet base.

"Oh…my God…"

"Lizzie, I know it's early, but I love you and I want you to be my wife. And I can't hold on to this ring anymore. It's been burning a hole in my pocket since I bought the damn thing."

He loved her? He *loved* her?

He'd never said that before, though she'd suspected it. What he felt for her had been in his eyes and his voice and his body. But she'd figured he might never actually speak the words just because self-expression was hard for him.

Yeah, well, not only had he let the Big Three fly, he'd backed it up with a serious piece of geology and a proposal.

Sean flushed. "Lizzie, I didn't mean to spring this on you. I just can't not ask. I go for what I want. It's my nature. And I want you—"

She fell to her knees in a rush of chiffon and threw her arms around him, crushing the ring between them. "Yes…yes…I'll be your wife…. I love you, too."

As his big body trembled a little, she got the impression he might have been a bit nervous.

"You know what, Lizzie?" He pulled back, slipped the ring onto her finger and held the diamond in place. "With you in my life, I'll always be out in the sun on a summer day beside the river. No matter where I am or what I'm doing, I'll always be happy."

She smiled through her tears. "It's the same for me."

"Good." He smiled and his South Boston accent came out in full force. "Because I love you there, Lizzie. Got it wicked bad for you."

She laughed and held on to him again. "I wouldn't have it any other way."

* * * * *

Look for Billy and Mac's stories,
coming soon.
Only from Jessica Bird
and Silhouette Special Edition.

Welcome to cowboy country...

Turn the page for a sneak preview of
TEXAS BABY
by
Kathleen O'Brien
An exciting new title from Harlequin Superromance
for everyone who loves stories about the West.

Harlequin Superromance—
Where life and love weave together in
emotional and unforgettable ways.

CHAPTER ONE

CHASE TRANSFERRED his gaze to the road and identified a foreign spot on the horizon. A car. Almost half a mile away, where the straight, tree-lined drive met the public road. He could tell it was coming too fast, but judging the speed of a vehicle moving straight toward you was tricky.

It wasn't until it was about two hundred yards away that he realized the driver must be drunk…or crazy. Or both.

The guy was going maybe sixty. On a private drive, out here in ranch country, where kids or horses or tractors or stupid chickens might come darting out any minute, that was criminal. Chase straightened from his comfortable slouch and waved his hands.

"Slow down, you fool," he called out. He took the porch steps quickly and began walking fast down the driveway.

The car veered oddly, from one lane to another, then up onto the slight rise of the thick green spring grass. It just barely missed the fence.

"Slow down, damn it!"

He couldn't see the driver, and he didn't recognize this automobile. It was small and old, and couldn't have cost much even when it was new. It was probably white, but now it needed either a wash or a new paint job or both.

"Damn it, what's wrong with you?"

At the last minute, he had to jump away, because the idiot behind the wheel clearly wasn't going to turn to avoid a collision. He couldn't believe it. The car kept coming, finally slowing a little, but it was too late.

Still going about thirty miles an hour, it slammed into the large, white-brick pillar that marked the front boundaries of the house. The pillar wasn't going to give an inch, so the car had to. The front end folded up like a paper fan.

It seemed to take forever for the car to settle, as if the trauma happened in slow motion, reverberating from the front to the back of the car in ripples of destruction. The front windshield suddenly seemed to ice over with lethal bits of glassy frost. Then the side windows exploded.

The front driver's door wrenched open, as if the car wanted to expel its contents. Metal buckled hideously. Small pieces, like hubcaps and mirrors, skipped and ricocheted insanely across the oyster-shell driveway.

Finally, everything was still. Into the silence, a plume of steam shot up like a geyser, smelling of rust and heat. Its snakelike hiss almost smothered the low, agonized moan of the driver.

Chase's anger had disappeared. He didn't feel anything but a dull sense of disbelief. Things like this didn't happen in real life. Not in his life. Maybe the sun had actually put him to sleep….

But he was already kneeling beside the car. The driver was a woman. The frosty glass-ice of the windshield was dotted with small flecks of blood. She must have hit it with her head, because just below her hairline a red liquid was seeping out. He touched it. He tried to wipe it away before it reached her eyebrow, though, of course, that made no sense at all. Her eyes were shut.

Was she conscious? Did he dare move her? Her dress was covered in glass, and the metal of the car was sticking out lethally in all the wrong places.

Then he remembered, with an intense relief, that every good medical man in the county was here, just behind the house, drinking his champagne. He found his phone and paged Trent.

The woman moaned again.

Alive, then. Thank God for that.

He saw Trent coming toward him, starting out at a lope, but quickly switching to a full run.

"Get Dr. Marchant," Chase called. "Don't bother with 911."

Trent didn't take long to assess the situation. A fraction of a second, and he began pulling out his cell phone and running toward the house.

The yelling seemed to have roused the woman. She opened her eyes. They were blue and clouded with pain and confusion.

"Chase," she said.

His breath stalled. His head pulled back. "What?"

Her only answer was another moan, and he wondered if he had imagined the word. He reached around her and put his arm behind her shoulders. She was tiny. Probably petite by nature, but surely way too thin. He could feel her shoulder blades pushing against her skin, as fragile as the wishbone in a turkey.

She seemed to have passed out, so he put his other arm under her knees and lifted her out. He tried to avoid the jagged metal, but her skirt caught on a piece and the tearing sound seemed to wake her again.

"No," she said. "Please."

"I'm just trying to help," he said. "It's going to be all right."

She seemed profoundly distressed. She wriggled in his arms, and she was so weak, like a broken bird. It made him feel too big and brutish. And intrusive. As if touching her this way, his bare hands against the warm skin behind her knees, were somehow a transgression.

He wished he could be more delicate. But he smelled gasoline, and he knew it wasn't safe to leave her here.

Finally he heard the sound of voices, as guests began to run around the side of the house, alerted by Trent. Dr. Marchant was at the front, racing toward them as if he were forty instead of seventy. Susannah was right behind him, her green dress floating around her trim legs.

"Please," the woman in his arms murmured again. She looked at him, the expression in her blue eyes lost and bewildered. He wondered if she might be on drugs. Hitting her head on the windshield might account for this unfocused, glazed look, but it couldn't explain the crazy driving.

"Please, put me down. Susannah… The wedding…"

Chase's arms tightened instinctively, and he froze in

his tracks. She whimpered, and he realized he might be hurting her. "Say that again?"

"The wedding. I have to stop it."

* * * * *

Be sure to look for TEXAS BABY,
available September 11, 2007,
as well as other fantastic Superromance titles
available in September.

The latest novel in The Lakeshore Chronicles
by *New York Times* bestselling author

SUSAN WIGGS

From the award-winning author of *Summer at Willow Lake*
comes an unforgettable story of a woman's emotional journey
from the heartache of the past to hope for the future.

With her daughter grown and flown, Nina Romano is ready to
embark on a new adventure. She's waited a long time for dating,
travel and chasing dreams. But just as she's beginning to enjoy
being on her own, she finds herself falling for Greg Bellamy,
owner of the charming Inn at Willow Lake and a single father
with two kids of his own.

DOCKSIDE

"The perfect summer read." —Debbie Macomber

*Available the first week of August 2007
wherever paperbacks are sold!*

REQUEST YOUR FREE BOOKS!

2 FREE NOVELS PLUS 2 FREE GIFTS!

SPECIAL EDITION®

Life, Love and Family!

YES! Please send me 2 FREE Silhouette Special Edition® novels and my 2 FREE gifts. After receiving them, if I don't wish to receive any more books, I can return the shipping statement marked "cancel." If I don't cancel, I will receive 6 brand-new novels every month and be billed just $4.24 per book in the U.S., or $4.99 per book in Canada, plus 25¢ shipping and handling per book and applicable taxes, if any*. That's a savings of at least 15% off the cover price! I understand that accepting the 2 free books and gifts places me under no obligation to buy anything. I can always return a shipment and cancel at any time. Even if I never buy another book from Silhouette, the two free books and gifts are mine to keep forever.

235 SDN EEYU 335 SDN EEY6

Name _____ (PLEASE PRINT)

Address _____ Apt. _____

City _____ State/Prov. _____ Zip/Postal Code _____

Signature (if under 18, a parent or guardian must sign)

Mail to the **Silhouette Reader Service™:**
IN U.S.A.: P.O. Box 1867, Buffalo, NY 14240-1867
IN CANADA: P.O. Box 609, Fort Erie, Ontario L2A 5X3

Not valid to current Silhouette Special Edition subscribers.

Want to try two free books from another line?
Call 1-800-873-8635 or visit www.morefreebooks.com.

* Terms and prices subject to change without notice. NY residents add applicable sales tax. Canadian residents will be charged applicable provincial taxes and GST. This offer is limited to one order per household. All orders subject to approval. Credit or debit balances in a customer's account(s) may be offset by any other outstanding balance owed by or to the customer. Please allow 4 to 6 weeks for delivery.

Your Privacy: Silhouette is committed to protecting your privacy. Our Privacy Policy is available online at www.eHarlequin.com or upon request from the Reader Service. From time to time we make our lists of customers available to reputable firms who may have a product or service of interest to you. If you would prefer we not share your name and address, please check here. ☐

SSE07

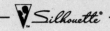

SPECIAL EDITION™

Look for

BACHELOR NO MORE

by *Victoria Pade*

Jared Perry finds more than he's looking for when he and Mara Pratt work together to clear Celeste Perry's name. Celeste is Jared's grandmother and is being investigated as an accomplice to a robbery, after she abandoned her husband and two sons. But are they prepared for what they discover?

Northbridge Nuptials

Available September wherever you buy books.

ATHENA FORCE

Heart-pounding romance and thrilling adventure.

Professional negotiator Lindsey Novak
is faced with her biggest challenge—to
buy back Teal Arnett, a young woman with
unique powers. In the process Lindsey
uncovers a devastating plot that involves
scientists from around the globe, and all of
them lead to one woman who is bent on
destroying Athena Academy...at any cost.

LOOK FOR

THE GOOD THIEF

by Judith Leon

*Available September
wherever you buy books.*

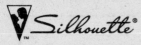

COMING NEXT MONTH

#1849 BACHELOR NO MORE—Victoria Pade
Northbridge Nuptials
Shock #1: Mara Pratt's sweet, elderly coworker led a double life—
decades ago, she'd run off with a bank robber and was now facing hard
time! Shock #2: The woman's grandson, corporate raider Jared Perry,
was back in Northbridge to help Grandma, and he saw Mara as a
tempting takeover target—trying to steal her heart at every turn!

#1850 HER BEST MAN—Crystal Green
Montana Mavericks: Striking It Rich
Years ago, DJ Traub had been best man at his brother's wedding to
Allaire Buckman—but secretly DJ had wanted to be the groom, so he'd
left town to avoid further heartbreak. Now the rich restaurateur had returned
to Thunder Canyon and into the orbit of the still alluring, long-divorced
Allaire. Had he become the best man…to share Allaire's life?

#1851 THE OTHER SISTER—Lynda Sandoval
Return to Troublesome Gulch
Long after tragedy had taken his best friend in high school, paramedic
Brody Austin was finally ready to work through his own feelings of guilt.
That's when he ran into his best friend's kid sister, Faith Montesantos.
All grown up, the pretty, vivacious high school counselor helped him
reconcile with the past and move on…to a future in her arms.

#1852 DAD IN DISGUISE—Kate Little
Baby Daze
When wealthy architect Jack Sawyer tried to "cancel" his sperm
donation, he discovered his baby had already been born to single
mother Rachel Reilly. So Jack went undercover as a handyman at her
house to make sure his son was all right. Jack fell for the boy…and fell
for Rachel—hard. But when daddy took off his disguise, would
all hell break loose?

#1853 WHAT MAKES A FAMILY?—Nicole Foster
Past betrayal and loss made teacher Laurel Tanner shy away from love
at every turn. And Cort Morente was hardly an eligible bachelor—he
was focused on rebuilding his own life, not on romance. But their
shared concern for a troubled child was about to bring them together in
ways they'd never dreamed possible.…

#1854 THE DEBUTANTE'S SECOND CHANCE—
Liz Flaherty
When journalist Micah Walker took over his hometown paper, the
top local story was former debutante Landy Wisdom. Domestic abuse
had left Landy broken—her selfless help for other victims had left her
unbowed. Could Micah give her a second chance at love…or would she
turn the tables and give *him* a chance—to finally find true happiness?

SSECNM0807